END OF THE TRAIL?

"Excuse me, ladies, I need to take a quick squint around. Hope we can resume this little chat shortly."

Fargo headed back toward the Ovaro. His plan was to ride in a wide loop, then scout the river bank on foot.

"Nobody asked you to come back, Fargo!" Mattie called after him. "Donner Summit was fifteen years ago. Progress has come to the West since then. We don't need your so-called help!"

Without looking back, Fargo opened his mouth to reply. But from the direction of the river, a rifle spoke for him.

The high-caliber report cracked like a giant blacksnake whip, echoing throughout the canyon in a hundred explosions.

There was no dramatic cry of pain, no arms flung skyward. As the horrified women watched, Skye Fargo's legs simply folded like empty sacks and he flopped to the ground hard, face-first. He lay there stone still—except for the gruesome sound of his toes scratching the dirt in several quick, jerky death twitches. . . .

THE
TRAILSMAN
#277

HELL'S
BELLES

by

Jon Sharpe

A SIGNET BOOK

SIGNET
Published by New American Library, a division of
Penguin Group (USA) Inc., 375 Hudson Street,
New York, New York 10014, USA
Penguin Group (Canada), 10 Alcorn Avenue, Toronto,
Ontario M4V 3B2, Canada (a division of Pearson Penguin Canada Inc.)
Penguin Books Ltd., 80 Strand, London WC2R 0RL, England
Penguin Ireland, 25 St. Stephen's Green, Dublin 2,
Ireland (a division of Penguin Books Ltd.)
Penguin Group (Australia), 250 Camberwell Road, Camberwell, Victoria 3124,
Australia (a division of Pearson Australia Group Pty. Ltd.)
Penguin Books India Pvt. Ltd., 11 Community Centre, Panchsheel Park,
New Delhi - 110 017, India
Penguin Group (NZ), Cnr Airborne and Rosedale Roads, Albany,
Auckland 1310, New Zealand (a division of Pearson New Zealand Ltd.)
Penguin Books (South Africa) (Pty.) Ltd., 24 Sturdee Avenue,
Rosebank, Johannesburg 2196, South Africa

Penguin Books Ltd., Registered Offices:
80 Strand, London WC2R 0RL, England

First published by Signet, an imprint of New American Library,
a division of Penguin Group (USA) Inc.

First Printing, November 2004
10 9 8 7 6 5 4 3 2 1

The first chapter of this book previously appeared in *Skeleton Canyon,* the two
hundred seventy-sixth volume in this series.

The Trailsman

Beginnings . . . they bend the tree and they mark the man. Skye Fargo was born when he was eighteen. Terror was his midwife, vengeance his first cry. Killing spawned Skye Fargo, ruthless, cold-blooded murder. Out of the acrid smoke of gunpowder still hanging in the air, he rose, cried out a promise never forgotten.

The Trailsman they began to call him all across the West: searcher, scout, hunter, the man who could see where others only looked, his skills for hire but not his soul, the man who lived each day to the fullest, yet trailed each tomorrow. Skye Fargo, the Trailsman, the seeker who could take the wildness of a land and the wanting of a woman and make them his own.

Hell's Canyon, the Northwest, 1861—
Where human devils hunger for female flesh, and a savage angel
named Fargo serves them only lead.

1

Skye Fargo had been following the women for nearly two days, trying to decide if they were crazy, drunk, or just hog stupid.

Close observation, however, finally made him conclude they were the greenest greenhorns he'd ever seen. And some of the shapeliest, all five of them. But they obviously had no concept whatsoever of the danger they were in.

An attractive, auburn-haired gal in a rose taffeta dress drove their celerity wagon, a lighter, cheaper version of the popular Concord coach. And she was doing a piss-poor job of it, Fargo told himself. She literally didn't know gee from haw.

No way in hell did she get that four-horse rig this deep into the gold-rich mountains of the Northwest without a guide who knew scouting and trail craft. Which might explain the male snakebite victim Fargo had buried just east of here in the rugged Bitterroot Range.

The man some called the Trailsman wasn't sure of the exact calendar month and didn't need to be, any more than he needed a watch. The slant of the sun told him the time, the bite in the air the season. He had headed far west just after the first big snowmelt, when the passes were no longer blocked by ice. Nights in the Rockies were still knife-edge cold, days that bracing kind of cool that almost tempted Fargo to shave off his beard just so he could feel the air stinging his cheeks.

He had crossed the Wind River Range through Jackson Hole and over Teton Pass. He then continued west over the dangerous Lolo Trail, used by the Nez Percés when heading east to hunt buffalo on the plains. Riding into the pristine beauty of the Northwest at this time of year was a natural tonic to Fargo. Another reason he had wandered out this far was to see if his old hunter and trapper friend, Snowshoe Hendee, was still above the earth.

But spotting the female-filled celerity wagon had diverted Fargo's attention and hooked his curiosity. For the past twenty-four hours the women had made no effort to leave their ill-chosen campsite in the Seven Devils Mountains beside the Snake River. And the reason was obvious: a snowmelt-swollen river ahead, and no trails behind that they could manage. They were trapped.

This was no country for a conveyance of that size, even in the hands of a capable teamster. The mania for establishing new roads and ferries, which Fargo saw sweeping much of the West, was frustrated this far north by long winters with temperatures reaching forty below zero. And the only "settlement" (so new that word was a stretch) was the overnight tent city of Lewiston, well north of here. The few roads just recently begun by the U.S. Army were abandoned as the gathering drumbeats of sectional warfare back East drew soldiers off the frontier.

Right now, though, Fargo noticed with sudden interest, four of the women didn't seem to have one damn care in the world—except for braving the shockingly brisk water of a mountain-runoff stream as they disrobed and plunged in for a bath.

"Now, at this point," Fargo remarked quietly to his Ovaro, "a gentleman would turn his gaze away."

A few seconds later, a grin tugged at Fargo's bearded lips. "Ain't no gentlemen west of Omaha." He kneed the pinto stallion forward for a better look at this free flesh show.

"Oh, my stars and garters, it's *frigid*!" cried out a petite beauty as she poked one toe gingerly into the burbling stream.

She wore only a muslin chemise tied off all the way up over her alabaster fanny, which glowed, in the afternoon sun, like fine ivory. The thick russet thatch covering her mound was a shade darker than the hair worn in a single braid over her left shoulder. She began to untwist the braid.

"Shoo, Tammy, you're just a little priss," teased a tall,

leggy blonde with a trace of Swedish accent in her musical voice.

She had long, pale-gold hair, long-lashed eyes of lavender blue, prominent Scandinavian cheekbones. Even less inhibited than Tammy, she had stripped buck. Fargo was forced to shift in his saddle as he took in those long, shapely legs, the taut little strawberries-and-cream caboose, the corn-silk bush and firm, high breasts with nipples turned into hard little bullets by the crisp spring breeze.

To cap the climax, she had an identical twin who was wading in right behind her, likewise naked as a newborn. Only now did Fargo spot one sure way to tell the twins apart. This second sister had a little crescent-shaped birthmark on her curvaceous right hip.

The pearly allure of the twins' skin was an exciting contrast to the flawless mocha flesh of the fourth woman who had wandered down to the stream to bathe. Fargo, who had been to New Orleans a few times, had already guessed she was most likely Creole, a mixture of French and Spanish blood. A pretty, fine-boned face with coffee-colored, wing-shaped eyes, all crowned by raven-black hair in coronet braids.

She had stripped down to her red satin corset and was idly unlacing it with one hand as she advanced, engrossed in a book.

Fargo rode to the edge of the screening timber, then reined in and swung down, leaving his brass-frame Henry in the saddle boot. Since graze was scarce and the Ovaro hungry, he put the stallion on a long tethering rein so he wouldn't wander into view of the women. But the hearty Ovaro, never spoiled by stall-feeding, was content to stand still and browse the juicy pine needles lying about.

"Girls, just *listen* to this," the Creole lovely called to her companions, her accent more French than Southern.

In a melodramatic stage style, she began reading aloud from her book. Her hand covered the title, but the author's name was Washington Irving.

" 'With his horse and his rifle, he is independent of the World, and spurns all its restraints.' "

Just as she mentioned spurning restraints, the Creole sighed audibly and wiggled out of her corset. Fargo admired her unblemished skin, the color of sunlit amber. In his vast experience, very few women could move with such catlike grace while bare naked—a fluid, seamless motion except for the swaying of impressive breasts.

"Hooboy! Right there's your problem, Yvette," Tammy taunted the Creole in a hill-country twang Fargo guessed was west Arkansas. "You're alla time lookin' for men like in them silly storybooks. *Hee*-roes, my sweet aunt! And you going on twenty-four years old? You best grab you a meal ticket before your tits drop. Just be happy if you can find one that can last more'n a minute in the saddle."

While Tammy delivered this sage advice, Fargo watched her bend forward from the grassy bank to suds and rinse her hair. The petite little hill girl's luscious butt yawned invitingly wide at Fargo, bold as the crack of day. The leggy twins, meantime, were lathering each other's backs, shivering and exclaiming at the cold. The fifth woman, the auburn-haired one who seemed to be in charge, remained up at the campsite.

For Fargo, it was a true embarrassment of erotic riches. But even now, when any red-blooded man under eighty had a damn good excuse for relaxed vigilance, Fargo's old survival instincts took over. These silly cottontails might not realize it, but danger surrounded them from several sources.

Still sheltered in dense brush, he reluctantly averted his gaze from the frolicking nymphs to closely study the surrounding terrain.

He was in the wild region east of the Blue Mountains and west of the Bitterroot Range, with Lewiston several days' ride to the north and the Boise River well south, just before the desolate lava-bed country began. Vast Hell's Canyon sprawled straight ahead of him, split by the Snake River. The canyon was aptly named. Ancient glacier scars pitted the landscape and made travel, especially by vehicle, truly hellish.

The area looked pristine and deceptively peaceful, at first glance. He watched the low, gliding swoop of an eagle searching for prey. Spruce forests and other conifers turned the surrounding slopes bluish-green, and at the higher elevations pure-white aprons of snow still clung to the granite peaks and rock plateau above the tree line.

4

Just then Fargo's concentration was momentarily broken by a feminine shriek. But it was only a chorus of jeers from the bathers. The twins were teasing Tammy for being afraid to enter the ice-cold water.

" 'Hang your clothes on a hickory limb, but don't go in the water!' " they chanted in unison. "That's fraidy-cat Tammy!"

"Oh, serve it on toast," Tammy retorted. She popped open a pink parasol to protect her fair skin from freckles while the wind dried her dark russet hair.

By now the twins were playfully wrestling over a lump of lye soap. Fargo, hot blood pulsing in his veins, watched their bodies grind together until they fell in a giggling, thrashing heap of bare limbs and perky bottoms. Yvette, apart from the others, stood in water up to her thighs, a dreamy expression on her face as she sudsed herself in slow circles, while her thoughts roamed far afield.

Fargo somehow forced his attention back to the surrounding terrain. It *looked* peaceful, all right. But this stretch of the Northwest had lately become a tinderbox. The trouble began in 1858 with a major gold strike up north along the Fraser River in British Columbia. Then gold was discovered throughout this stream-rich area in 1860. Violence and lawlessness were widespread and inevitable given two undeniable facts: Gold was why men were here, and whatever they found, or robbed, they carried with them.

But bad as all that was, Fargo had noticed another source of festering tension: White prospectors were staking out tomahawk claims—girthing trees to kill them and mark their diggings. Problem was, they were staking their claims on forbidden Nez Percé reservation land.

In past years Fargo had been cordially received at the Nez Percé village nearby, on the Clearwater fork of the Snake. But in the last few days he'd seen signs that several local tribes were especially busy knapping flints to make arrow points—plenty of them.

So it was finally time to confront these pretty tenderfeet with the truth. Either they lit a shuck toward civilization, and in a puffing hurry, or they were marked for carrion bait—if not worse.

"Don't be scared, ladies," Fargo called to the startled beauties as he stepped out into the open. "The name's Skye

Fargo. I'm a mite rough-looking and ripe from the trail. But I'm lovable as a newborn kitten."

He flashed a toothy smile as he touched his hat to the shocked women. Their separate reactions were telling—and quite promising.

The twins stood exposed but modestly cupped their hands over their breasts. Yvette, the Creole beauty, plunged her entire body under water up to her neck. But she couldn't pry her eyes off the new arrival. Tammy, her honey-colored gaze sparking to life at sight of this tall, buckskin-clad interloper, stood up boldly. She wanted him to see all of her petite but alluring body. The sheer, wet muslin was nearly transparent and nicely emphasized the plum circles of her nipples.

Tammy was also the first to recover from the surprise. She flashed Fargo a kittenish smile. "Well, ain't *you* the sassy one, Mister Skye Fargo?"

"Sassy as the first man breathed on by God," he assured her. "Only, not *quite* so pious."

Yvette, Fargo noticed, had wasted her time by trying to hide in the crystal-clear mountain water—her lithe, lovely form was clearly visible. In fact, a fish always looked bigger underwater—and so did a set of high-grade tits.

"*M'sieur* Fargo, your eyes!" she exclaimed. "Right now I feel that I am gazing into a bottomless blue lake high, high in the mountains. You *are* the rugged frontier type just like Captain Bonneville, *mais oui*."

"Don't know the gent," Fargo apologized. "Cavalry?"

"Oh, don't mind her, Mister Fargo," Tammy said. "Captain Bonneville is the hero in a story book she's reading. Yvette fancies herself an actress from New Orleans, thinks you can eat ideas and swap dreams for cash."

Tammy's man-hungry eyes feasted on Fargo. "But me? I'm Tammy Lynn Jones from Fort Smith, Arkansas, and I don't find my men in books. Them silly blondes gawking at you is the Papenhagen twins from the Nebraska sand-hill country."

"I'm Hilda," said one of the twins.

"I'm Helga," said the other, the one with the crescent birthmark.

"Hilda, Helga, pleased to meet both of you."

Right then, however, Fargo realized the little skinny-dipping party was about to come to a screeching whoa. The auburn-haired woman had spotted him and was hurrying down the slope from their camp, her face a sternly pretty mask.

"That's Mattie Everett," Tammy supplied quickly. "Sorta in charge of us. Nice enough sometimes, but pushy and likes to get on her high horse."

"Sir, what *are* you doing here?" Mattie demanded as she drew up in a huff. "Hilda, Helga! Shame on you two! Get some clothes on! You, too, Yvette and Tammy. You girls are acting like Santa Fe harlots."

She was a few years older than the other women, Fargo noticed, and like them a damn fine looker. There was also more worldly experience in those pretty brown eyes than her high-hatting manners let on. And it wasn't a corset, he realized, that gave her the hourglass waist and flat stomach. His eyes lingered there, picturing her naked.

"I also have a face," she told him sarcastically.

"Yes, ma'am, and *it's* mighty easy to look at, too."

What were the odds, Fargo thought idly, that on the woman-scarce frontier, all five of these gals would just happen to be pretty and fetchingly built? Hell, most men out here were grateful for any female with a few teeth left.

"Mattie, this is Skye Fargo," Tammy put in quickly.

"May I ask why you're here, Mr. Fargo? Or would that question be too obvious, given the bare flesh surrounding you?"

"Good thing I am here," Fargo assured her. "*Some*body has to watch over you pretty pilgrims. No offense, Mattie, but you gals are so green you didn't even think to find the lee side of the cold night wind when you camped last night. Hell, a rabbit has that much sense."

Angry red spots appeared on her cheeks. "Watching over us? Just plain watching us, you mean."

"Well, I've already confessed to the others how I wasn't Bible-raised," Fargo admitted in a hale, cheerful tone. "Matter fact, Mattie, I'm a pagan pure and simple. But when I see prime ladies like all of you, I *do* believe in heaven. And, angel? I'm not looking away from a naked goddess unless she tells me to."

"My stars!" Tammy exclaimed. "Not only a randy stallion, but a charmer, too. First dibs, girls."

Mattie whirled toward Tammy and the others, fists balled on her hips. "Push those thoughts right out of your mind, Tammy Lynn. We're *all* spoken for already, and we've even signed contracts. Say, didn't I tell you girls to get dressed? And as for *you*!"

She turned back toward Fargo, eyes blazing. "You're still staring at them?"

"Why, hell, yes. Nobody's told me to stop."

"Stop!"

Fargo grinned amiably. "Sure—soon as you put it to a vote. I'm a true democrat, and the rest don't seem so offended as you."

Mattie sputtered some angry retort, but Fargo missed it. He had been watching an eagle hovering and gliding out over the Snake. Only, at the moment it was veering sharply to the west, flying full-bore away from the river.

Moments later, several crows did likewise.

"Excuse me, ladies, I need to take a quick squint around. I suggest you get into less, ahh, exposed locations. Hope we can resume this little chat shortly."

Fargo headed back toward the thick stand of brush and jack pine where he'd left the Ovaro. His plan was to ride in a wide loop, then scout the river bank on foot.

"Nobody asked you to come back, Fargo!" Mattie called after him. "Donner Summit was fifteen years ago. Progress has come to the West since then. We don't need your so-called help."

Without looking back, Fargo opened his mouth to reply. But from the direction of the river, a rifle spoke for him.

The high-caliber report cracked like a giant blacksnake whip, echoing throughout the canyon in a hundred explosions and spooking the team horses up at camp.

There was no dramatic cry of pain, no arms flung skyward as if in angry protest at dying. As the horrified women watched, Skye Fargo's legs simply folded like empty sacks and he flopped to the ground hard, face-first. He lay there stone still—except for the gruesome sound of his toes scratching the dirt in several quick, jerky death twitches.

2

A shocked, breathless stillness followed the last twitch of Skye Fargo.

Then, uttering a horrified cry, Yvette began a melodramatic swoon. But she stopped herself, as if remembering this was not a French Quarter theater. She started toward the fallen man, but waist-high water slowed her down.

"Stop, you feather-brained fool!" Mattie snapped, leaping into the water to grab her charge by the wrist. "You saw what happened just now when Fargo got too far out into the open. Stay below the curve of the bank, or you might be next. He looks dead, anyway. He can wait."

"Dead? Merciful heaven!" Hilda cried out. "Is it Indians attacking? Oh, Mattie, *is* it savages?"

"Of course not," Mattie said. "Now, just settle down. The Indians in this area are not killers or . . . ravishers of white women. Mr. Chandler made that abundantly clear in his advertisement and telegrams."

"Well, *somebody* sure is a killer," Tammy said, peeking up over the sloping bank. "And yonder comes a fella, his gun still smoking."

A man in a black slouch hat was trotting a big sorrel gelding toward them from the dense wall of trees and hawthorn bushes crowding the bank of the Snake. A wisp of blue smoke did indeed curl from the muzzle of the huge rifle that lay across his thighs like an iron pole.

"Son of a *bitch*, what have I done?" the man cursed as he rode up. "Pardon my French, ladies. But I swear on Granny's grave that was a mistake. A god-awful mistake, yessir. Jesus Criminy! I mistook his buckskins for an elk's hide, I surely did."

9

The seventeen-hand sorrel splashed easily through the stream, and the man reined in beside the inert form of Skye Fargo.

"Damn careless of me. I feel just awful, I surely do. But I fear he's got to be dead. A Sharps Big Fifty generally kills even with a wing shot. Poor bastard. Let's roll him over anyhow and see if he at least died with his eyes shut. I will not abide a staring corpse."

The man slid his Big Fifty into a rawhide saddle sheath before he swung down, spurs chinging, to squat near Fargo. He grabbed one muscle-corded shoulder and rolled him roughly onto his back.

But the "poor bastard" was only possum-playing. Fargo's right fist was already filled with steel. He shoved the muzzle of his Colt hard into the man's crotch and thumbed back the hammer with an audible click. The new arrival quickly stood up but wisely didn't try to flee.

"Ladies," Fargo called out, "you ever seen a rooster turned into a capon? It's mighty quick work."

The man had the small, mean face of a terrier. His slouch hat was filthy and covered with burn marks where it had doubled as a pot holder.

"Jee-zus Christ, mister! You scared the snot outta me. Man, you done a bang-up job of playing dead. Now you've had your little joke, why'n't you leather that shooter?"

The man flashed a big, servile smile full of teeth stained molasses brown. But Fargo had recognized this cur's type instantly. At heart he was a coward. But behind most cowards was a brooding discontent that could instantly become murderous rage.

Fargo said, "Wipe that grin off your map, back-shooter, we ain't pals. 'I feel just awful, I surely do,' my ass."

The Trailsman came agilely to his feet. There was a new hole in his buckskin shirt and a warm, itching line of mild pain where the ball had barely kissed his right rib cage.

"Back-shooter? Now, ease off on that talk. I just mistook your buckskins for an elk's hide, honest to Christ I did, mister. Hell, I got no quarrel with you. Don't even know you."

Fargo knew such mistakes happened constantly on the frontier. He himself had once almost pulled the trigger on a buckskin-clad Northern Cheyenne, mistaking him for a

10

deer. But that had been at twilight in a forest. This just now was in broad daylight, with Fargo in the open. Which made the man's claim a convenient way to turn murder into "death by misadventure," especially in this lawless territory.

"Elk?" Fargo repeated. "You're poor shakes as a liar, mister. Sure, east of here there's plenty of elk, deer, antelope, buffalo, you name it. But the biggest game you'll tag around here is wild turkey, because there's damn few licks. That's common knowledge hereabouts."

Fargo had seen salt licks—self-impregnated earth surrounding saline springs—draw game in fantastic numbers. But people in this salt-deprived region would starve if not for the industrious Mormon pack-horsemen from Utah farms.

"No licks? Hell, that's news to me. I'm new to these parts. The name's Baker. Tim Baker. I was a wolfer out in west Kansas; now I've come out to the high lonesome to pan gold. I do wish you'd move that Colt 'fore it ruptures me. You've no cause—"

"Your mouth runs like a whip-poor-will's ass," Fargo cut him off. "A wolfer from Kansas, huh? And I s'pose you used *this* to skin 'em with?"

With his free hand Fargo pointed to the cutthroat razor worn in a leather sheath on the man's belt. The straight razor was a favorite weapon of night-riding gold thieves, who liked to kill their victims silently in their bedrolls.

"I do some barbering, too," the man replied, his horse trader's eyes shifting to all sides.

Fargo grinned with his lips only, his eyes ice-cold and dangerous. "Uh-huh. And I teach ballet classes. Frankly, old son, I don't figure your word is worth a cup of cold piss."

Despite his predicament, anger sparked in the man's eyes. "That's twice now you called me a liar."

"Since you're keeping such close score, I also called you a back-shooter."

"Around here that's cemetery talk."

Fargo nodded, winning the staring contest. "It is, ain't it? Way I see it, kill one fly, kill a million."

The women watching and listening didn't fully grasp the lethal meaning of this last exchange. But both men knew

11

precisely the serious significance of what had just transpired.

Fargo always riled cool, because on the frontier it was often deadly to get into even a minor quarrel. The code was tolerant on many points, but once a direct insult was issued, there was no hedging. One man calling another a liar meant one of them would die.

"All right," Fargo said. "It's clear where me and you stand, bushwhacker. The only reason I don't kill you right now is I lack proof. But you'll make your play again. And next time, I'll shoot you to rag tatters."

The man's smirk was only half formed before Fargo wiped it off quick with several fast, hard slaps.

"We got one point to clear up," Fargo said, "before you dust your hocks out of here for good. Like all stupid men, you can't lie worth a damn. Tim Baker is one of your summer names. Now I want your real name, and I'm watching your snake eyes *real* close, slick."

"I told you. It's Tim Baker."

Fargo shook his head, wagging the Colt for emphasis. "You're too stupid to ever four-flush me. Now, you got one last chance to spit it out. You lie this time, I'll kill you for cause and let the buzzards bury you."

"It's Jack Duran," the man said from a face twisted with hate.

Fargo nodded. "Good. I like to know who I'm going to be having my cartridge sessions with. Now raise dust."

"Oh, the death hug's a-comin', all right," Duran promised as he stirruped and swung into leather. "But, mister, you got no idea on God's green earth what you just stepped into. Yessir, the death hug's a-comin', it surely is."

Fargo kept Duran covered until the rider and his mount were swallowed up by the dense growth near the river. By the time Fargo crossed the little stream and returned his attention to the ladies, he was disappointed to see they'd obeyed Mattie—all were at least partially clothed.

"I take it," he said to Mattie, "you're the one ramrodding this . . . uh, outfit?"

"If that means I'm in charge of the welfare of these four ladies, yes."

"No offense, but you need an experienced trail guide.

And frankly, you're so green you couldn't locate your own lovely ass at high noon with both hands."

Her eyes blazed with indignation. But Fargo thought, Let her stew. He'd seen firsthand how ignorance was deadly out West. He had watched too many pilgrims go under because they didn't bother to learn anything about the country they were crossing. They would find an easy stretch of river, perhaps, and conclude the entire river must be easy to navigate—after all, it was that way back home in Ohio or Maryland. And now the West was filling up with names like Bloody Bones Canyon and Skullcrush Rapids.

"We're doing just fine, thank you, Mr. Fargo," Mattie retorted.

"Like hell you are. May I ask where you *think* you're headed?"

"That's none of your—"

"Chandlerville," Tammy piped up, her voice excited. "Mattie's got her a map, says it's real close by—"

"Hush, Tammy," Mattie Everett cut in. "This man doesn't need to know our business. He's not the law—he has no authority to question us."

"That's right. And I say let everybody go their own gait," Fargo assured her. "That's why I held back from hailing you. I wouldn't be prying, Mattie, if I didn't know for a fact you ladies are in some deep trouble out here. You talk about law? There *is* none this far west except lynch law. No marshals, no soldiers, no circuit judges or backcountry courts. You saw that jasper just now try to plug me—this area's thick with his type and dirty plays like that. And there's no Chandlerville."

"You got that last part wrong, Skye," Tammy butted in.

"*Oui, m'sieur,*" Yvette echoed. "Chandlerville is a thriving western town. There are even spas and opera houses."

"Spas and opera houses," Fargo repeated, stunned by how gullible folks could be. "And ice cream and oysters, too, huh?"

He stared at Mattie, his eyes narrowing in speculation. "I take it this nearby, thriving town of Chandlerville is named after the same wise Mr. Chandler you quoted on the Indian situation hereabouts?"

"Oh, yes." One of the twins (Fargo couldn't tell them apart when they were dressed) spoke before Mattie could.

"Mr. George H. Chandler of Beacon Hill in Boston. A graduate of Harvard and founder and mayor of Chandlerville."

"He speaks five languages fluently and once played Hamlet in college," Yvette added on a sigh. "A man of culture and sensitivity."

"And Mattie's gonna marry up with him," Tammy boasted. "And the rest of us is getting hitched to big shots in the business community."

"Business community," Fargo repeated, shaking his head in utter amazement at human folly—and human treachery. "So you're mail-order brides? Well, one way or another you're being snookered, ladies. Snookered real bad. You'll find no Chandlerville or any other 'town' within hundreds of miles of here. Unless you count Lewiston, which is all tents and brush huts."

"You must be mistaken, M'sieur Fargo," Yvette insisted. "The town must be close by."

"Sorry, pretty lady. Not even a fly speck of a settlement. Matter fact, you'd need to go all the way to Astoria on the Oregon coast to find one. And don't look for an opera house there, neither."

Digesting all this, the four younger women began protesting, their faces concerned and confused. But Mattie, Fargo noticed, only looked angry about his interference. That made no sense unless she knew something the others didn't.

"Girls!" she spoke up sharply. "We don't know this man, who calls himself Fargo, from Adam. Can't you see he has his own obvious reasons for wanting to take charge here? *Lustful* reasons?"

Fargo laughed. "Cold day in hell," he assured her, "when Skye Fargo has to use devious tricks to get under a gal's petticoats. No need to steal what is given freely. And I'll tell you this much—you're full of sheep dip if you think there's a town anywhere near here."

She tried to interrupt, but Fargo spoke over her.

"This place surrounding us is Hell's Canyon. Those peaks at your back are the Seven Devils Mountains. Northeast from here are Hell's Half Acre Mountains. We're not far from Lost Valley and the River of No Return. Do those cheery names sound like they'd pull in the opera crowd?"

Tammy's confusion was shading over into anger as she stared at Mattie.

"I ain't taking his side, Mattie. But if the town is so close by, why hasn't someone come to fetch us on in? That Jack Duran fella was just some drifter trash with filthy fingernails. Mr. Chandler wouldn't send riffraff like him."

"You forget," Mattie replied, "that Mr. Chandler provided an experienced wagon conductor for our journey from St. Louis. Obviously, he expects Mr. Shoemaker to bring us. How could he know the man would disappear?"

"This Shoemaker," Fargo said. "Your 'wagon conductor'—was he a short, husky man with a reddish beard and a goiter?"

"Why, that's him," Yvette said. "Luke Shoemaker. We last saw him four days ago when he rode out to locate water. Do you know him?"

"Just long enough to bury him. Rattlesnake dropped off a rock ledge, bit him on the neck. He couldn't suck out the venom, and with the bite so close to his brain, it put him down quick."

"Rattlesnake?" Yvette scooted out of the tall grass. "Perhaps, Mattie, *M'sieur* Fargo gives good advice? It is too dangerous to linger here."

"We aren't lingering," Mattie snapped. "Eventually someone from Chandlerville will notice we're stuck here."

"Lady," Fargo marveled, "you're stubborn as a rented mule."

"Maybe," Tammy suggested, batting her eyelashes at Fargo and twirling her pink parasol, "me 'n' Skye could ride in and tell 'em?"

Fargo smiled at her. "We can take a ride. But not to Chandlerville. It doesn't exist."

He looked at Mattie. "Let me tell you what does exist around here. For starters, in this season, unpredictable weather. It can drown you, freeze you, or smother you in snow, all without warning. And then there's a murdering road gang that's preying on prospectors and pack trains."

"So what? The weather seems fine to me. As for the

rest of it—do we look like prospectors or a pack train, Mr. Fargo?"

"No, you look much more valuable than either to women-starved desperadoes. How much food you carrying?"

"Most of it's gone," Mattie admitted. "We're down to hardtack and beans, a few potatoes."

"And when that's gone? Starvation is a prime killer in these parts. There's no roads or transportation, no local farms, and poor hunting. The nearest farms are in Utah, but right now the Mormon pack trains are being slowed down by white road gangs and the local Indian troubles."

"Indian troubles?" one of the twins echoed, her big blue eyes growing wide with the fear planted by lurid dime novels. "But Mr. Chandler told us—"

"Your Mr. Chandler is either a damned fool or a bigger liar than Benedict Arnold."

Fargo waved an arm around, encompassing the entire area. Eager men with pans and rockers, no less fervent and greedy than the original forty-niners, were fanning out into Hell's Canyon and the hills near the Boise River. Rich diggings were also reported on the Salmon River. Now the famous placer camp motto was heard everywhere: "Cash in and get out."

"This area is laced with creeks that show color," he said. "Problem is, plenty of 'em are on Nez Percé land off-limits to whites. They got their new reservation just last year, and most prospectors haven't heard or don't give a damn. It doesn't help that a few corrupt chiefs are stirring up the pot by taking bribes for allowing prospecting."

Mattie's tone was growing more impatient. "Mr. Fargo, be all that as it may, surely the Nez Percés know we five women are hardly prospectors bent on hurting them? I've heard from various sources that they are friendly toward whites."

Fargo nodded. "Usually that's true. This area isn't near as dangerous as the Dakota Territory, far as Indians. But the Nez Percés are less predictable right now because of these prospectors and because they're at war with the Flatheads. And the Nez Percés have two kinship tribes in this area, the Wallawallas and the Palouse. Some of them are on the scrap against whites, too."

Fargo paused to give emphasis to his next point. "These tribes are mostly good people, in peacetime. But you *don't* want to get caught up in Indian warfare. Female prisoners are valid trophies. And a female scalp is highly prized for its thicker, longer hair."

This time his point sank home, even to Mattie, who paled slightly. Both twins unconsciously raised a protective hand to their long, lustrous blond hair.

"Well, what are you suggesting?" Mattie demanded. "That we just turn around and go back?"

Fargo shook his head. "Bad idea. We're all lucky we made it through the Bitterroot Range on our way out. There's Flatheads at war just east of here, too, battling the Blackfeet tribe. Way I see it, you got only two choices."

"Which are . . . ?"

"I guide you northwest to Fort Walla Walla or south to Fort Bridger. I'd recommend Walla Walla, 'cause there's Bannocks and Shoshonis to the south, no boys to mess with. Both forts are U.S. Army; they'll have safe lodgings for women. You can make arrangements from there to get back East, maybe with a returning supply convoy."

Mattie stubbornly shook her head. "We've got no choice, Mr. Fargo, but to remain right here and wait for help from town. We have contracts to honor."

Honor . . . Fargo searched Mattie's attractive but worldly face and told himself, again, here was trouble. She was dealing from the bottom of the deck. All well and good, except that four other women were being placed in grave danger by her duplicity.

"Suit yourself," Fargo said. "But this is a free country. I aim to camp nearby and keep an eye on you ladies until this thing gets settled. I'm curious to see this 'help from town.' "

"This thing *is* settled, Mr. Fargo," Mattie bit off in an acid tone. "It's none of your damn business."

Fargo grinned before he spun on his heel to return to his stallion, catching Tammy's eye. "Well, Mattie, I'm the pushy type that likes to stick his nose into the pie."

Tammy grinned back, catching his innuendo and liking the sound of it. Whatever insults Mattie hurled after him, Fargo ignored. His mind was back on Jack Duran. Fargo had watched carefully when the stone-cold killer rode out, and the Trailsman's well-honed sense of smell had picked up a scent of wood smoke in that direction. Now he intended to make a thorough search west of the Snake.

The problem of Mattie Everett and her secrets could wait. You can't clean out rats, Fargo told himself, until you first locate their nest.

3

"I like to shit strawberries when he stuck that shooter in my jewels," Jack Duran reported to his boss. "I don't know who that jay is, but he's got hard twist writ all over him. And it 'pears to me he means to jump claim on our females. Told me to clear away from there and don't come back. No sign of Shoemaker anywhere."

"S'at so?"

For a moment Ace Ludlow's hard-bitten eyes turned so angry they looked like molten metal. He had thinning red hair, a jagged slash of cruel mouth, and the self-satisfied manner of despotic men of power.

"Then that'll cost him dear," he pronounced like a judge passing sentence. "Those four other gals, hell, he's welcome to a quick taste. But he's got my woman, too. My private stock that no man sees naked and lives to boast about it. You don't come 'tween *this* dog and his meat."

Ace, Jack Duran, Fatty McGratten, and Hoyt Jackson formed the original core of Ludlow's ever-expanding gang of murderers and thieves now taking advantage of the new-found bonanzas in the Northwest. The four men were scattered around a solid, roomy cabin well chinked with clay and wooden wedges so it was snug even in winter.

Built by French Canadian trappers working for the North West Company, the cabin was secure and, for such a wild region, comfortable. It even included a mud-daubed chimney rising from a stone hearth. Corner shelves of crossed sticks held a few crockery dishes, and oiled-paper panes in the windows let in some filmy yellow light.

"So what the hell's the problem?" demanded Fatty McGratten. "We finally lure us some woman flesh alla way out here back of beyond. Some *fine* quiff, Jack says. And we're gonna let one noble crusader buffalo us? Christ sakes, we ain't back in the States, boys. We don't gotta worry 'bout a buncha damn badge-toters buttin' in. Let's ride over there right now, settle his hash, and grab our women. I'm needin' to plant my carrot, and mighty damn soon. Hoyt's mare is starting to look good to me."

Nobody laughed because Fatty wasn't joshing. Nor was he at all fat, but rail-thin, tall, and slope-shouldered. Bland and inoffensive to look at, he was in fact a stone-hearted killer like every man in Ace's gang. He wore no belt gun, only a hand ax in a sheath. He had spent years learning to throw it with unerring accuracy, and he could split a running man's skull into two equal halves at thirty yards.

"See? Right there, Fatty, is why I'm ruling the roost," Ace retorted. "On account I'm the only one around here ever uses his think-piece. The problem ain't this stranger. Hell, killing one man will be chicken-fixin's. The problem is how to handle this thing without drawing attention to the location of this cabin. This place right here, chappies, is the key to the mint, and we all know it."

The cabin, not far from the Clearwater fork of the Snake River, was indeed an ideal hideout. It had deliberately been built with Indian threats in mind. The place was well disguised in a seemingly impenetrable gully of brush and thickets. Surrounding brush was so thick a man couldn't penetrate it without a hatchet, and then only slowly. The place was actually entered and left by a long tunnel whose entrance was well hidden in a cut bank near the Snake. The only man who knew of its existence, a former partner of Ludlow's, was long dead.

"Lucky thing for us this area is starting to swarm with sourdoughs," Ace pointed out. "That means easy pickings. But Fatty wants us to go riding out in broad daylight, toss a wall of lead at this stranger, then fetch our women kicking and screaming back here. All it takes, with all that racket and movement, is for one man to drop spyglasses on us, and see us come back here."

Ace slashed one hand through the air, the Cheyenne cut-off sign that symbolized one was speaking of the dead. The others got his point.

"Boys," he continued, "we've made plenty of widows

and orphans in this area, and we've got the gold beneath the cabin floor to show for it. It's also all the proof needed to make sure we stretch hemp. And in gold country, that means drag-hanging behind a horse. Can't you see the risk if we lose our discipline now? This thing's got to be done right. Discreet like."

While he spoke, Ace reigned like an unshaven monarch in a horsehair-stuffed chair, his feet propped on a nail keg. The gang had their pick from items discarded along the Oregon Trail. His trio of hand-chosen lieutenants sat on split-bottom chairs and three-legged stools.

"Discreet?" Hoyt Jackson repeated, his face and tone belligerent. A swarthy, heavyset man with hairy hands, he and Fatty were playing poker with a greasy deck of cards. "Ain't we gonna kill him?"

Ace came to the feather edge of exploding in rage, then wisely checked himself. Much as he hated diplomacy, it was needed these days. Besides his three companions, there were several more men asleep behind a partition made from horse blankets, and more yet out on sentry duty.

Many of the unsavory types flocking to join Ace's gang had fled far West to beat the rope. Others were self-exiles, especially from Missouri, Arkansas, and Kansas, who wanted no part of the war talk brewing back East. Only a fool, they reasoned, died for anything but a chance to get rich quick with no hard labor involved. Ace welcomed their firepower. But the way they were suffering from boredom and cabin fever, he knew any one of them might snap and kill him at any moment. Even one of these three. So he was forced to curb his tongue.

"Are we going to kill him?" Ace repeated. "Hoyt, does a whore have wrinkled bedsheets? He's got our poon, ain't he? Sure as hell I want him dead, dead as a Paiute grave. I'm just saying this ain't like when we was taking scalps down in Mexico with nobody to butt in. We can't all ride out and turn our guns loose on that bearded bastard. In fact, we won't even bust a cap. We'll wait until later. Near dark, Fatty can sneak into throwing range and split his brain pan open."

"Nah, t'hell with that," Duran snapped. He stopped cleaning his Big Fifty long enough to stroke the cutthroat razor on his belt. "He's *mine*, that smug son of a whore.

He gelded me in front of all them women. Now it's personal between me and him, and I mean to settle accounts when I slice him open from neck to nuts."

Katy Christ, Ace told himself, it's worse than he'd thought. Jack Duran was always moody and mad-dog mean, but Hoyt had rarely ever challenged Ace as he had just a moment ago. Ace knew he *had* to get some woman flesh in here, and quick, or the gang would disintegrate—after killing him.

Sure, this was easy money lately. Killing drunk, exhausted prospectors in their sleep was a cinch bet, especially with silent specialty killers like Fatty and Jack along. But that meant lying low by day, and these remote living conditions were damn hard. And criminals, by and large, were men who craved the creature comforts.

The shortage of good tobacco and liquor, the monotonous diet of jerked beef and beans—these were hard enough. But the severe lack of women was worst of all. Ace, like many of his day, believed in the "volcano theory" of manhood: A man needed regular release or he would explode.

"Jack," he replied with all the patience he could muster, "don't you see it's important now to just get it done quick, no delays? After all the work me and Mattie done to bamboozle these pert skirts, why risk lettin' this stranger wise them girls up? What, we should hold off just so's you can plant him to settle a grudge?"

"What's the big hurry?" Duran said. "He got the drop on me before I even mentioned who I was or why I was there."

"Don't matter," Fatty chimed in as he sorted out his discards. "Ace is right. That Chandlerville story is mighty thin stuff. This intruder could start prying into the facts. What if he mouths it around? The prospectors got 'em a new vigilance committee combing this area for us. They might get wind of it. Best if I just end it tonight."

"I s'pose," Duran conceded, still stewing. "But if you muff it, he's mine. What I don't get, what the hell's he nosing in for? It's no skin off his ass what we do with them gals."

"You chucklehead, it's the skin on *their* asses he's 'nosing' into," Ace said. "You blame him? Outside of a few smelly squaws, ain't no quiff nowheres near here. Why, up in Lewiston? White whores is making five hunnert a *night*, mister, and them's gals over forty."

"Then maybe I'll pull stakes and head to Lewiston," Duran carped. "Old gals is still gals. They also got decent grub there, at least. Christ, I'd give a fist-size nugget for a frosted cake."

Ace shrugged. "Don't let the door hit you where the good Lord split you."

His hard, glittering eyes met those of all three of his minions. Diplomacy or no, he still had to be the boss.

"That goes for every man jack one of you," he added. "You can stick or quit, it's all one to me. Just think on this, though. One, we're raking in the gold hand over fist. And two, soon as we snuff this crusader's wick, four fine females with bouncy tits will be spreading their legs for you boys back in the sporting parlor any damn time you feel like gettin' your ashes hauled."

The "sporting parlor" was Ace's name for an extra room connected to the cabin by a dogtrot or covered breezeway. It was originally built so trappers could keep their packs of smelly pelts separate from their living quarters during the long winter hole-ups.

Right now, however, it was scrubbed clean and housed little besides four crude wooden bedsteads with feather mattresses. All it lacked were the female sex slaves.

It was the darkly brooding Jack Duran himself who finally broke the tension with a grin. "Bouncy tits, huh? Hell, like they say at cowboy grub pile: Take all you want, but eat all you take."

The rest laughed with him, including Ace. His gunbelt was draped over one arm of the chair. Ace slid his Paterson Colt five-shot revolver out of the holster and palmed the cylinder to check the loads. He handled the weapon gingerly, for it had a "deadline" trigger—all the slack had been deliberately removed by shortening the sear. Thus he gained the fractional advantage in a showdown.

"Now you're whistling," he told Duran. "Jack, since you was the one who eyeballed this stranger good, you ride out and tell the sentries what he looks like. Fatty, run a whetstone over that tossin' ax. A little later, me and you will go pay him a visit, give him a splitting headache."

*　　*　　*

Before he rode out to scout the surrounding terrain, Skye
Fargo took the precaution of helping the women move
their camp to a higher slope with more exposed approaches. Mattie Everett raised hell about it, but Fargo
wanted them where he could keep an eye on them, or anyone riding in, from his present position down on the flat
tableland near the river.

At the moment, despite Mattie's assurances they were
safe, he had no intention of leaving those women unpro-
tected. Fargo could read hard cases as well as he could
read trail signs. Jack Duran, and others of his ilk siding
him, would be back.

The man definitely was not a sourdough as he had
claimed. His clothing, pale skin, and soft hands proved that.
So there was no other reason to be here—except for the
reason suggested by the razor on his belt.

Such thinking reminded Fargo to constantly send a cross-
shoulder glance toward the women's campsite whenever a
break in the foliage allowed.

The westering sun felt good on his back and shoulders
as Fargo slowly rode in ever-widening circles along the east
bank of the snowmelt-swollen Snake, his eyes in constant
motion. Broken brush, hoof-flattened grass, old embers or
horse droppings or cigarette butts—Fargo missed nothing.
His keen eye for detail was a long-established habit. Men
who failed to remain alert and observant on the frontier
usually met a hard and early death.

Fargo found more signs of Indians than whites. And
though he never relaxed in Indian country, he knew things
were generally calmer here in the Northwest—at least until
quite recently. Tribes like the Utes, the Modocs, and the
Nez Percés had entered into amiable commerce with
Americans, Spaniards, the British, the French, even the
Russians decades ago.

But now the "glittering yellow rocks" had been found in
this region and the fools were rushing in—with murdering
parasites like Jack Duran on their heels.

Fargo reined in beside a calm backwater of the Snake
and threw the bridle so his Ovaro could drink. When the
stallion had tanked up, he nudged his velvet muzzle into
Fargo's neck. Fargo fondly scratched the pinto's withers.

Over butte, plain, scarp, or valley, the stalwart Ovaro had never failed him.

"Well, old warhorse," Fargo said as he stirruped and swung up onto the hurricane deck, "let's see if we can find a gravel ford and scout the other bank for a piece."

The Ovaro was a strong swimmer, and that's how they'd cross if they had to. But Fargo didn't like the look of the fast-moving, swollen river. He knew the opaque water hid dangerous snags and sawyers—mats of congested driftwood that protruded from the banks and caused furious boils.

He searched in both directions along the bank, at times leading the Ovaro by the bridle reins through dense thickets. They emerged from a tangled deadfall, and Fargo felt a grin tugging at his lips.

"See? Seek, and ye shall find," he told the Ovaro.

A crude but strong ferry, made from two dugout canoes joined by logs, was tied to a tree root along the bank. A sturdy guide rope, tied to elm trees on both banks, stretched across the brawling, splashing river.

Fargo glanced around for the owner, but he didn't want to give a shout and announce his presence. Spotting no ferryman, he began to untie the mooring rope.

He flinched violently when a rifle suddenly spoke its deadly piece. A geyser of dirt kicked up, not three inches from his busy hands.

"Shit, piss, and corruption!" roared out a gravely voice from behind him. "Happens you want the use of that-'ere ferry, you sneakin' barnyard rat, you'll make medicine first with the hoss what owns it. And *that* would be me."

Fargo recognized the speaker by his distinctive and powerful voice even before he turned around to confront him.

"Snowshoe Hendee, you damn ornery old piker! You ain't gone under yet?"

There was a fast, furious crackling of brush as Fargo's old friend, mounted on a swaybacked mule, hurried out of hiding to see who was giving him the hail by name.

"Damn my eyes, it's Skye goldang Fargo! Cut off my legs and call me Shorty! Skye, you son of a bitch, this child is glad to see you still sassy!"

The grizzled old trapper was one quarter Apache through his dam. Hawk-nosed, with fierce, dark eyes, he had a wild tangle of frizzled gray hair and a silver beard worn in two braids. His walnut-wrinkled face attested to many decades spent weathering the elements.

"Gone under, you say?" he roared at Skye in a boastful tone. "Augh! Why, this hoss can *still* kill and skin ary grizz with one hand and shake the dew off his lily with the other! I'll outdrink, and outfight any pilgrim half my age! I can still shoot a squirrel's eye out every pop, and my pecker is so damn big there's still snow on it in July! Gone under? Fargo, don't *make* me thump you, you mouthy pup!"

By now Fargo's grin stretched ear to ear. Nothing had changed about the cantankerous old former mountain man since Fargo last broached a bottle with him in friendship. He was still a shameless boaster and liar who smelled like he was a long way from his last soap bath. But behind that bravado, Fargo knew, was also the iron backbone of a uniquely American pioneer from the shining times.

Fargo first met the old salt years earlier, when Snowshoe was a trader at the frontier post of Nacogdoches—down toward the Spanish Lake, as Snowshoe called the Gulf of Mexico. Long before that he was an adventurous Comanchero, one of the enterprising traders who trafficked directly with Comanches in defiance of Mexican law. And back in the heyday of the Rocky Mountain Fur Company, Snowshoe had trapped with the likes of Jedediah Smith and Willian Sublette.

"Snowshoe Hendee operating a ferry?" Fargo roweled him. "What, you a flatlander now, putting down roots?"

"Ahh!"

Still impressively spry, Snowshoe tossed a leg over the horn of his saddle and took out his plug, gnawing off a corner. When he had it juicing good, the Nor'wester said, "Folks is consarn stupid, that's all. It's a goldang shame, Skye. Nobody wants beaver hats no more. The furriers in St. Louis all want them damn nutria skins shipped up from South America. Big damn rats is all they are."

Snowshoe spat an amber streamer into the high grass of the river bank. "Hell, this child knowed Caleb Greenwood, the first mountain man. Knowed Manuel Lisa and Ezekiel Williams. Hell, it was *this* hoss what helped Lisa get the first license from the chilipep gum'ment to trade with the Pawnee. It makes me ireful now, all these damn grangers

26

acting like they own ever' damn raccoon what crosses their back forty."

Snowshoe's fresh-sounding anger always made it seem like only yesterday the long hunters were still making their beaver in truly free country. But Fargo saw the changes beginning with the end of the fur-trapper era in 1850 or so. More and more, the independent free trappers were forced to pay tribute to the giant companies.

By 1858 the Army had acquired Fort Bridger, Utah Territory. By then Fargo had watched the mountain men (except for determined old flints like Snowshoe) shift from trapping to the booming business of guiding and supplying Western emigrants.

Fargo nodded toward the mule. "I see you're still riding Ignatius. Figured you'd eat him by now."

"He'll eat me first. That animule is just like me—still has his full quota of original sin. Anyhow," Snowshoe said, "what brings you snoopin' and sniffin' around Lewis's River? Just the usual tormentin' itch to push on? Never knowed a man to have jackrabbits in his socks like Skye Fargo."

Snowshoe still called the Snake "Lewis's River" in honor of Meriwether Lewis.

"Actually, female troubles bring me here," Fargo replied sarcastically.

Briefly, he explained the situation with the five women stranded here in Hell's Canyon and the earlier visit from Jack Duran.

"You been burning any wood lately?" Fargo asked. "I caught a scent of wood smoke earlier, in this direction. Same general path Duran rode out, too."

Snowshoe nodded. "Ain't heard that name. This child don't truck much with others. But I'd wager I've seen him. Others, too. There's signs of an organized gang everywhere around here, plain as bedbugs on a clean sheet. But none of 'em uses my ferry. So they got their own ford somewheres or their hosses is all strong swimmers."

Snowshoe paused to dig a tick out of his scalp. Fargo moved upwind of him. The odor he gave off would cower a cavalry regiment.

"Now, as to that smoke smell," Snowshoe resumed,

"that's a poser. This child has noticed it plenty, too, but ain't seen no camp nor dwelling. But there's more pilgrims comin' in lately, building fires."

Fargo nodded. "Could be nothing. But they've got to have a hideout near here, someplace where they're laying up by day."

"A-huh, absodamnlutely. But I ain't never seen it. 'Course, ain't looked, neither. The Flatheads got 'em a saying: 'Don't go searching for your own grave.' These boys you're tracking now, Skye, is death to the devil. But you got another nut-buster of a problem on your hands: Ruck-a-Chucky is back in these parts, stirring the pot to a boil."

"Oh, *hell*. Up to his usual tricks?"

Snowshoe nodded, grinned, spat amber, then howled with mirth, almost rolling off the bowed back of Ignatius.

"Damn straight, and it's a corker this time. That sly red grifter has set hisself up as a Nez Percé 'chief' hereabouts. Even stuck a piece of shell through his nose. Been putting his 'X' on worthless contracts that let whites prospect on Injin land."

"That damned fool," Fargo muttered.

"Fool, huh? He's hauling in the money nine ways to Sunday. But he's also helped to draw sourdoughs onto rez land like flies to syrup. Happens the Nez Percés catch him, they'll flay Chucky's soles."

"A Nez Percé chief?" Fargo repeated. "Hell, he's got more Modoc blood than Nez Percé. He's named for the Ruck-a-Chucky Falls in California. That's where I first met him."

Snowshoe was still chuckling. "I know, ain't it a hoot? But Injins all look alike to most pilgrims. 'Sides, they don't care if he's Ben Franklin's bastard idiot just so's they got 'em a paper to wave around, make it look legal like."

Fargo mulled this new information. He considered Ruck-a-Chucky a highly entertaining acquaintance more than a friend. The profiteering, irreverent Modoc could try a man's patience to the point of aggravation with his various schemes. Fargo had pulled his bacon out of the fire when Ruck-a-Chucky was caught salting mines in the High Sierra and faced a lynch mob.

Maybe, Fargo concluded, *I should have let him swing.* This grift he was now running—it was luring in more prospectors, thus giving more incentive to the gold-camp killers like Duran.

But it could also lead to a bloodbath among whites if the Nez Percés were pushed too far. Peaceful by nature, the tribe could be formidable once they greased for battle.

"I better palaver with him," Fargo decided. "He owes me a favor. Can you locate him and bring him to see me? I don't dare wander too far from those women."

Snowshoe nodded. "I can fetch him by to see you tomorrow. 'Bout late forenoon?"

"All right." Fargo checked the slant of the sun and decided to scout the opposite bank of the river another time. He'd been away from camp long enough.

As he took his leave of Snowshoe, Fargo recalled Jack Duran's threat from earlier: *The death hug's a-comin'.*

4

By the time Fargo returned to the camp overlooking the eastern rim of Hell's Canyon, the sun was going low and the wind had developed a cold, raw edge. This was the season, in the Northwest, when temperatures varied as much as thirty degrees between balmy days and near-freezing nights.

"Any trouble?" he called to Mattie Everett as he rode up, his slitted gaze carefully scanning the surrounding terrain.

"Not since you left," she replied tartly. "Now you're back, I imagine there'll be more. You seem to attract it, Mr. Fargo."

"No misdoubting that."

Fargo swung down and began stripping the neck leather from his Ovaro. "So . . . you still waiting for that trail guide in a top hat to arrive from Chandlerville, are you?"

"Smirk all you want to," she blazed at him. "I assure you this will all be settled and settled soon. Maybe then you won't be so glad you stuck around."

Fargo watched her from thoughtful eyes as he stripped off his saddle and spread the sweat-soaked blanket in the grass to dry in the wind.

"If I was the sensitive type," he replied in his mild way, "I might take that as a threat."

Mattie ignored him. She was kneeling beside a three-legged iron kettle, stirring supper. She wore a split-buckskin riding skirt with a crisp white shirtwaist that flattered her fine figure. The lustrous auburn hair was drawn back in a neat coil. And those fancy side-buttoned ankle shoes—she hadn't been wearing those this morning, either.

Seems mighty gussied up, Fargo thought, for a gal that's about to turn in. Like maybe she was expecting someone. . . .

Fargo received a much warmer reception, however, from the other four women. Tammy, busy nearby peeling the last of the potatoes they'd brought along, watched him with a sly come-hither gaze in those honey-colored eyes. The Papenhagen twins, Hilda and Helga, sat on the padded driver's seat of the celerity wagon. They were brushing each other's long golden tresses.

Their smiles for Fargo were a little shier than Tammy's, but no less warm and welcoming. And Yvette, the stunning Creole beauty from New Orleans, couldn't pry her bewitching amber eyes off this striking example of "the frontier rustic."

Regretfully, Fargo turned his attention back to Mattie as he began rubbing the Ovaro down briskly with handfuls of grass.

"You're right it'll be settled soon," he told Mattie. "Like I said this morning, you got a choice to make. Northwest to Fort Walla Walla; south to Fort Bridger. I'll guide you ladies to one or the other, and I recommend Walla Walla."

"We're not going to *either* Army post, Mr. Fargo. We'll wait right here for our—our fiancés to find us and take us to Chandlerville."

"All right," Fargo said. "Meantime, you got a close neighbor. Because I'm not drifting on until I eyeball these 'fiancés.' *You* may know damn well what's going on here, Mattie, but those other four girls are walking blind into a trap of some kind."

"My lands, Mr. Fargo, you horny males will even hide your lust behind shows of 'nobility,' won't you? Either that, or you are as silly and melodramatic as Yvette. There *is* no trap."

"So you say. But you also say there's a 'thriving community' near here called Chandlerville, and I know that's pure swamp gas. But let's say you're on the level, you really do believe in this Rocky Mountain El Dorado. What's your plan if I ride off, like you want, and nobody comes for you?"

"Why, we're not helpless. We have a team—"

"Not for long you don't if you keep treating them the way you are."

Fargo pointed toward the team of four big blood bays, taking off the sparse grass nearby.

"This morning, before I rode out, I pried stones out of their hoofs and found one festering thorn. In country like this, your horse dies or comes up lame and you're buzzard bait."

"Our guide, Mr. Shoemaker, took care—"

"He's dead," Fargo reminded her bluntly. "Another thing: During daylight, always try to tether your team farther out from camp. That way there's graze near camp when you bring them in at night for security. You're slowly starving them."

"What is this, Professor Fargo, the first day of frontier school?" Mattie jabbed. Again Fargo detected an almost hysterical fear just beneath the surface of her scorn.

"You sure-god need it," he assured her, "because frankly, lady, you don't know cow pie from apple butter about survival."

He nodded toward the celerity wagon. The harness, traces, and tug chains were all tangled in a mess around the double tree.

"You'll require an hour just to sort that out. And it's a stupid way to treat the equipment you count on to stay alive."

By now the rest of the women had come in closer, lured by Fargo's no-nonsense tone and manner.

"How you ladies set for weapons?" he asked next.

"Weapons?" Yvette repeated, as if the word were Chinese.

"I got one," Tammy said.

With a rustle of petticoats, the petite, shapely woman went to the celerity wagon, returning moments later.

"My pa give me this when I left Fort Smith," she said, handing Fargo an ancient flintlock musket. "His grandpa used it to fight the Redcoats. Pa is just a poor hoe-man, never had no money to buy a new rifle."

The weapon was old, all right, but Fargo noticed it was in excellent repair. Tammy also had a powder flask and a large leather pouch filled with patches and one-ounce lead balls.

"Beyond a few yards, these old muskets are damned inaccurate," Fargo said. "But the noise and smoke will sometimes spook Indians and horses. And if you do hit your man with a musket ball, you'll be able to drive a steam engine through the hole it makes in him. Know how to use it?"

Tammy nodded. "Pa showed me."

"If you ever do fire it during a scrape, be damn sure to pull the ramrod out first. In the heat of battle, it's easy to forget."

Fargo glanced around at the others. "That's it?"

"Of course that's it," Mattie replied. "We came West to get married, Mr. Fargo, not to shoot people."

"Why, Mattie!" Yvette exclaimed. "You keep a pistol under the seat of the wagon. The one you said you bought in St. Louis. I've seen it."

Mattie's eyes shot daggers at the Creole. Fargo walked over to the celerity wagon, climbed up onto the box, groped under the seat. He returned with a Colt Navy .36-caliber six-shot revolver.

"Nice weapon," he told Mattie. "Walnut grips, even. Buy it new or secondhand?"

"Why . . . new," she replied. She added hastily: "Of course, I've fired it a few times for practice."

"Uh-hunh. Mattie, tell me, what's the difference between a revolver and a pistol?"

"How would I know?"

"What caliber is this weapon?"

"Mr. Fargo, I don't know calibers from cabbages."

"How long you had it?" he pressed.

Mattie bristled at this interrogation. "I don't know, a few months. What's the difference?"

"I find it a mite peculiar, don't you, that you say you bought this weapon new a few months ago, yet this model was manufactured *ten* years ago, in 1851."

She flushed. "It's easy to rook a woman in a gun shop, I suppose."

Rook. Criminal slang . . . There was a word Fargo seldom heard law-abiding ladies use.

"Either you bought this weapon secondhand," Fargo told her, "or someone gave it to you. Hell, you don't even know what ammo it takes."

"What is this?" Mattie demanded. "The Inquisition?"

She snatched the weapon back from Fargo. "I do not appreciate all of these nosy questions."

"Yeah, I see that," Fargo said, meeting her eyes.

For a moment, before she turned away from his probing stare, Fargo felt a cool prickle on the back of his neck: For several seconds, the muzzle of the loaded gun had been pointed right at his belly.

"*Damn,*" Ace Ludlow cursed in a low tone. "Ain't no way in hell we're getting closer until the sun goes alla way down. He musta moved their camp from when Jack was here earlier. That bastard ain't wearing them buckskins just for eyewash, Fatty. He's got real trail savvy. He's put them women in a perfect defensive position. We move in any closer until after full dark, he'll spot us."

The two men had flattened themselves behind a low hummock perhaps five hundred yards from the campsite. There was no more cover beyond this point, just the grassy lower slope of one of the Seven Devils. The sun was only a ruddy afterthought on the western horizon, but too much light remained to move in yet.

Fatty McGratten never wore a belt gun, only his beloved and deadly throwing ax. But he was a fair shot with the Volcanic Arms lever-action repeating rifle that lay in the grass beside him.

"Too bad we didn't bring Jack's Big Fifty," he said. "We're out of range for my rifle, but I could plug him right now with that Sharps."

"Nix on that talk," Ace snapped. "Moon's in full quarter, and with that clear sky there'll be plenty of stars out tonight. You got the night vision of a cat. You're going to kill him silently with your ax. That way, see, when the cottontails find him dead in the morning, it's just one more anonymous gold-country murder. It ain't linked to us."

Fatty snorted. "Christ, boss, them she-critters will find out damn quick just what sorter 'brides' they're gonna be. Why the kid gloves?"

"Already t-told you why," Ace replied, teeth chattering against the gathering chill of the night wind. He pulled out his hip flask and tossed back a bracer, handing the flask to

Fatty. "We ain't got them penned up in the sporting parlor yet, *that's* why. We blow this meddling stranger to perdition right in front of them, you think those high-strung, flighty females will just skip alongside us back to the hideout?"

"Hell, no," Fatty admitted. " 'Cept for Mattie, they'll screech and caterwaul and make enough racket to wake snakes."

"The way you say, chum. And gunshots just add to the risk we'll be spotted heading in a big group toward our hideout. The key is to come and go in ones or twos, and make sure we don't raise a stirring-and-to-do anywheres near that cabin."

Ace patted the scattergun lying beside him. Usually he relied on his Paterson Colt, with its special deadline trigger. But this double-ten shotgun was his special bodyguard, reserved for extreme situations. Both shells were loaded with coins, and a point-blank blast would literally cut a man in half; two men, if they were standing close to each other.

"There'll be no gunplay unless things go to hell," Ace explained. "We want to show up tomorrow as respectable gents ready to help damsels in distress."

"Oh, by the Lord Harry, they're damsels sure 'nuff," Fatty said, his voice husky with lust. "Mattie done good work."

Ace's mean, hard face went so tight it looked skullish. "She always does. She knows what'll happen if she don't."

Ace owned a retractable spyglass he had taken off one of the prospectors he had murdered. He and Fatty had both ogled the soon-to-be sex slaves.

"Me?" Fatty said. "First off, I'm climbing all over both them blondes."

"I plan to top every damn one of 'em every damn day," Ace boasted. "You boys know my only rule: Mattie is branded stock; my brand. Nobody else touches her. The other four? Hell, it's first come, best served."

Ace extended his spyglass and brought Mattie into focus again. He felt his anger and frustration approaching a boil as he studied his woman. For many years she had learned to fear and obey him, to do his bidding in bed or in crimes. He could ruin her *and* her highfalutin family with one letter to a newspaper, and she knew it.

Right there she was. Like ripe fruit dangling inches out of a starving man's reach. *Christ*, he needed a woman with a desire like hell thirst.

But Jack Duran was right. This bearded man was a good one to respect. In fact, Ace had a troubling hunch he'd heard of this man before. The Ovaro, the Henry rifle, the buckskins, and that unnerving gaze that seemed to see things other men couldn't—this just might be the wandering horsebacker some called the Trailsman. Of course, legends were always bigger than the actual man.

Then again, Ace reminded himself, the actual man looked pretty damn big.

But he glanced at the darkling sky, and his jagged slash of cruel mouth twisted even meaner. This Trailsman was a big man, all right. But in just a little while, Fatty McGratten's lethal ax would literally cut him down to size.

"Skye," Tammy said, "what was you doing out there in the grass with that twine and them sticks?"

"Making a rabbit snare. With a little luck, tomorrow you'll have something a little heartier than watery potato soup for supper."

Fargo had indeed been making a snare. But that was also an excuse to study the terrain thoroughly one last time before nightfall. He had noticed birds swerving in flight to avoid a line of hummocks to the left of, and below, the camp.

It could mean nothing. But Fargo had stayed alive all these years by always assuming potential danger was real danger.

"Potatoes," he repeated, shaking his head at the foolishness of tenderfeet.

"Why not potatoes?" Mattie demanded. "They keep well, and they're easy to cook."

"When meat is scarce, corn is the best food to take along," Fargo insisted as he tossed a handful of wild onions into the simmering pot. He had found them earlier by the river. "You can roast it on the cob, then leach it with ashes to make hominy. With just two rocks, it's easy to pound into johnnycake meal. Parched corn'll store for years and feed horses and men. But then, I guess feeding horses doesn't concern you much."

"Mr. Shoemaker said not to bring corn," Mattie retorted. "Said the savages would steal it for *their* horses."

"That's prob'ly why Shoemaker is dead," Fargo told her. "Because he didn't know so much as he thought he did. Indians never spoil a horse by graining it. Hell, they don't 'feed' their mounts, they let them fend for themselves. Their ponies can live on tree bark if they have to. I've even seen 'em chew shingles off a shack."

"Besides, they are *not* savages," Yvette chimed in passionately. "Captain Bonneville calls them 'untutored bachelors of the forest.'"

Fargo had to bite his lip to keep from laughing outright at the hero-hungry city girl.

"Hon," he said to her kindly, "all those romantic stories are dandy for whiling away a rainy day. But don't confuse books with life. Out here a gal needs a backbone, not a wishbone."

"*M'sieur* Fargo, you are so wise!"

"Nah, I'm too sinful and ornery to be called wise. I just own a lot of old scars from lessons learned in the school of hard knocks."

Yvette was hero-hungry, all right. But also man-hungry, Fargo realized, aware of the way she kept coquetting with him.

"Perhaps I could see these scars sometime?" she said, charmingly forward.

"Ain't *you* the brazen hussy all of a sudden?" Tammy snapped. "I called first dibs on him. *You* got Captain Bonneville, remember?"

"Girls," Mattie interceded. "See it? You're letting this man drive a wedge between you. I'm warning you not to fall for that seductive smile of his. He's trouble."

Again Fargo got the distinct impression that Mattie was scared. Not scared by the situation she was in, but rather of some human threat hanging over her.

He let his gaze travel around the circle of women in the rich, mellow glow of the last of the day's sunlight. None of these gals, Mattie included, looked hard and careworn enough to call a crib gal. But neither was any of them likely to be a virgin or a blue-nosed prude. And *all* beauties. As if carefully selected to fit an order.

The twins looked especially fresh and pretty in robin's-egg blue gingham dresses with lace flounces. They were both dutifully cleaning their gleaming white teeth with splayed willow twigs.

"They do *every*thing together," Tammy whispered in his ear. "Even go out in the weeds to pee together. Betcha they'll both share each other's husbands, too. Heck, maybe all four of 'em'll end up in one bed."

Tammy giggled at her own suggestion.

"That'd be a lot of butts bumping together, wouldn't it?" she added.

Fargo grinned, gazing with a new perspective on the twins. They did *every*thing together, huh? . . .

"That it would," he agreed wistfully.

Suddenly jealous, Tammy's voice turned peevish. "*They* ain't got nothin' I ain't got, there's just two of them is all. But you can only enjoy one at a time, anyhow."

"Dumplin'," Fargo assured her when he finished laughing, "in my books, you play second fiddle to *no* woman."

She lowered her voice. "I know things, too, Skye. Like how to make a man feel real good. I mean, *real* good. My men get real loud, Skye, I make 'em go so wild."

Fargo didn't take on this wet-nursing job just to get his wick dipped. But if a woman was above the age of consent and below the age of indifference, he was always happy to fill the aching void in her life.

Tammy's lustful talk and urgent, hungry tone had aroused him. Enough light remained for her to spot the impressive furrow she'd raised in his trousers.

"Laws!" she exclaimed, but almost in a whisper so the others couldn't hear. "That's a real pants-buster, fella. Did *I* do that?"

"It sure's hell wasn't the butter-and-egg man."

"I ain't one to tease a man—not a man like you, anyhow. Let's do something about it, all right? Real soon . . . please?"

"I'll be camping right close by," Fargo assured her. "If you need *any*thing, I'm a light sleeper."

"I'll be waking you up," she promised.

The short and scattered pockets of grass forced Fargo to leave the Ovaro on a long tether. As he kicked in the picket pin, he again sent a slanted glance toward those hummocks below, barely visible now in the grainy twilight.

The wind was brisk, so Fargo quickly gathered up some rocks and built a low, Apache-style windbreak. By the time he had spread his groundsheet and blankets behind it, a butter-colored full moon was visible in a sky infinitely sprinkled with bright stars.

He lay his Henry rifle and Arkansas Toothpick where they'd be ready to hand. Then he opened the loading gate of his Colt and rolled the cylinder to check the chambers. Satisfied all was ready, Fargo stretched out fully clothed and waited for the clue that the next battle had arrived.

Fifteen minutes or so slid by, a half hour, and during all that time Fargo heard only the lonely whistling of the wind and the steady hum of insects.

And then, all in a heartbeat, the insects fell silent and Fargo knew he had his clue.

Once again Death was closing in on him, even as he sprang into action.

5

"Like shootin' fish in a barrel," Fatty McGratten gloated in a whisper. "Hell, who even needs a full moon when the dumb bastard is hunched over a fire?"

"Stop b-battin' your gums and get it done," Ace hissed in his ear. "I'm fuh-freezin' my oysters off. And the way that wind keeps shifting directions, his stallion might catch our scent."

Privately, Ace wasn't feeling as confident as Fatty about "the dumb bastard." It had been a long, tiring crawl up the slope until Fatty was finally in easy throwing range. Ace had expected darkness to force them even closer despite good moonlight.

But almost as if to oblige them, the stranger had built himself a small warming fire. Ace could clearly see him from behind, in outline, crouched over the tiny fire to capture its warmth. His back presented an inviting target.

Just one more silent, nocturnal murder like scores of bedroll killings Ace and his gang had perpetrated in the new gold diggings of the lawless Northwest. Yet, this time something felt off-kilter to Ace.

In fact, this setup seemed *too* inviting.

Sure, it was a chilly night, so the fire itself wasn't suspicious. Ace hated cold himself. He had grown up in the blistering heat of deep Texas and wouldn't have come along tonight if this job wasn't so important. But what nagged at him—the man would be warmer if he simply rolled up in his blankets and conserved body heat: a choice any sane man might prefer after almost being bushwhacked earlier today.

So Ace, sniffing a possible fox play, made sure both his

scattergun and his short iron were handy. Fatty was a superb killer, but not all that sharp at reading character. Ace figured stupid men were good for bullet bait anyhow, so let Fatty draw first fire in case the stranger was up to something.

Ace had faith in his field howitzer, as he called his coin-loaded shotgun. But if Fatty went under and he had to use it, there went any attempt at secrecy. Half of Hell's Canyon would hear the blast. But that lanky, woman-hogging intruder would be strewn in so many pieces they'd have to bury him with a rake.

Ace watched Fatty rise cautiously to his feet and slide the hand ax from its sheath on his belt. As was his ritual, he raised it gently to his lips and kissed the helve like a priest kissing his stole.

"Stranger," he whispered, as he cocked back his muscle-corded right arm, "here comes Death to cover you with a blanket."

Fatty followed through, released, and the ax *fwipped* end over end in a blurred, streaking line to its target. There was a fast *thwap* of impact, a feral cry of pain, and the stranger fell to one side, motionless.

"Huzzah! Didja hear the dollar drop in the box?" Fatty boasted. "Boss, I split that cockchafer like a stove-length!"

"Good throw, but keep your damn voice down," Ace muttered. "The women ain't camped too far away. Remember, we don't 'rescue' them until tomorrow."

Fatty chuckled. "Shoo! After they find their bodyguard split in two, they'll *beg* us to get them clear of here."

"That's the gait. We'll lie, tell 'em the killer could still be prowling around after them. That'll give us a perfect excuse to slip them back to the cabin one at a time, keep a low profile. Let's get back to our horses."

"Hang on, boss. I ain't leaving a good throwing ax," Fatty said. He picked up his Volcanic repeater from the grass and racked a load into the chamber. " 'Sides, I can swap that Henry of his for whiskey, and his boots look to be about my size."

"Well, get a wiggle on," Ace said impatiently. "It's c-colder than a landlord's heart."

Fatty knew he had struck his man dead-center with a solid blow, almost surely severing the spine. Even if he hadn't, that death cry told the story—the blade surely had chewed deep into the man's vitals, severing arteries and veins along the way. Nonetheless, Fatty moved in on cat feet, his rifle cocked and ready.

The buckskin-clad body lay near the fire. The obscene contortion of the limbs was typical in sudden, violent death. But as Fatty drew closer, his eyebrows began to tent in a frown.

"What in blue blazes?" he whispered.

The weak glow of the fire showed an unexpected and unnerving sight. The "body" on the ground was in fact only a buckskin suit stuffed tight with grass!

It's a damn scarecrow, Fatty told himself, baffled.

But his body grasped what his terrified mind couldn't admit. His bladder reflexively emptied in fear, and his heart leaped into his throat. He started to turn and run.

From the darkness behind a low stone windbreak nearby came the metallic snick of a hammer being cocked.

"You so much as twitch a muscle, mister," commanded a voice that clearly brooked no defiance, "and you'll be walking with your ancestors."

Fargo had expected gunshots, not a blade killer. Nonetheless, he had had enough presence of mind to cry out when the ax struck his decoy.

Using his extra set of buckskins had proved shrewd, and now he had the tall, rail-thin man dead to rights. Normally, the murdering intruder would just be dead. Fargo wasted no time asking questions of any man who tried to kill him in cold blood.

But there were other lives on the line here, and a rat's nest to sniff out. A prisoner, no matter how stubborn, would talk in a hurry once his ribs were wrapped in wet rawhide strips and he was staked out in the hot sun while the strips dried and shrank.

So Fargo hoped to trap this snake alive. But he made one miscalculation: He didn't allow for a second man so close by.

The moment Fargo issued his terse command, that second man was warned. A hammering racket of gunfire erupted out of the darkness below Fargo's little camp.

A fusillade of bullets buzzed past his position like blowflies.

He could easily spot the orange bursts of muzzle fire from a handgun. But before Fargo could pivot, drop a bead, and return fire on the hidden shooter, the prisoner opened up with the small-caliber but fast-action repeating rifle.

High on Fargo's list of dangers to always, *always* avoid was crossfire. Cursing himself for a careless fool, he tucked one shoulder in and rolled hard, performing several somersaults and coming up on his heels fanning the hammer of his Colt.

His would-be assassin redirected his fire. For what seemed an eternity to Fargo, but was in fact only several heart-stopping seconds, both men flung lead at each other in the dim light. Finally Fargo's fourth or fifth shot tagged the rifleman in the base of the throat.

The man staggered hard, dropped his rifle, and collapsed to his knees. Fargo heard the ghastly gurgling sound as the man choked on his own blood.

But by now the other man had redirected his aim, too, and the covering fire from downslope was unrelenting. Figuring the skinny intruder was out of the fight for good, Fargo snatched up his Henry from the grass and dropped into an offhand kneeling position. Levering and firing rapidly, he opened up in the direction of those spitting orange streaks of muzzle fire.

The Henry's tube magazine held sixteen rounds, and Fargo was able to establish a withering return fire. The well-oiled ejector mechanism clicked flawlessly, raining shell casings all around him.

Just then, however, two things happened almost simultaneously: Fargo saw a sudden movement from the corner of his left eye, and heard, from the direction of the hidden shooter, the menacing and unmistakable double click of shotgun hammers being cocked.

The nearby movement was the mortally wounded man, somehow on the verge of exacting bloody revenge. Incredibly, he had managed to retrieve his throwing ax and lurch toward Fargo, thick ropes of scarlet blood spuming from his shattered throat.

Fargo, however, feared even more what was a mere eyeblink away. With a desperate, stretching dive, he managed to leap behind his little stone windbreak with no time to spare before two express-gun barrels exploded with a concussive roar that vibrated the air like thunder.

Fargo had no idea what kind of projectiles were loaded in those shells. But it sure's hell wasn't buckshot or bird shot. The blast hit his windbreak with a metallic racket that reminded him of artillery shrapnel raining in. Some of the outer stones were pulverized, and rock chips flew stinging into Fargo's eyes and face.

Then he saw the brunt of the shotgun blast broadside the staggering man who wielded the ax. In the generous moonwash, Fargo watched, repulsed and shocked, as the walking dead man was literally sliced to pieces by the lethal load.

Whatever the second man was shooting at him, Fargo decided to respect it. He was content to wait, hunkered behind his partially destroyed windbreak with Henry to hand, until he finally heard the swift rataplan of escaping hooves.

"It's all right, ladies!" Fargo shouted down toward the women's camp. "Sorry to disturb your slumber. The fireworks should be over for tonight."

The first thing he did was check to see that his stallion and the team horses were still grazing, unharmed. Then Fargo hauled his saddle, bridle, and bedroll to a new spot well away from his old camp—not only for security, but because he had no desire to sleep anywhere near the scattered spray of his attacker's remains.

That's one shotgun, Fargo vowed, I don't ever want to stare at.

Tomorrow the carrion birds and ground scavengers would feast on this spot. Except for one body part, the man's fully intact head, which had remained unscathed above the raggedly severed neck. Picking it up gingerly by the hair, wincing in disgust, Fargo dropped it into a burlap bag he took from a saddle pannier.

The carrion birds would get the head, too, all in good time.

In fact, Fargo even meant to make a sort of ceremonial offering of it.

*　　*　　*

"*Psst!* Skye? Skye, don't shoot me nor nothin'. It ain't trouble like earlier. It's just Tammy coming to see you."

Fargo was a light sleeper. But at the moment he heard the whisper, he was dreaming about Tammy. She was straddling his lap naked while the Ovaro galloped beneath them, bouncing her up and down on Fargo's shaft. So the voice, he figured, must just be part of his fine dream.

"Doggone you, Skye! You moved your bedroll. I nigh froze my hinder off looking for you. Now you best warm it right back up."

This time the voice was so close he felt warm breath tickling his eyelids, and smelled a fragrant, clean girl scent like honeysuckle and lilacs, plus that slightly heady, musky odor of female desire.

"Mmm," Fargo replied to his dream lover, stirring in his cozy, warm blankets.

"Well? You lettin' me in your blankets 'r not? You awake, Skye? I got something all tingling and ready for you, darlin'. I been a naughty girl, been getting myself warmed up for you. Feel . . ."

A soft hand took his callused one, and Fargo's eyelids rolled lazily open.

The moon was pale and wafer thin now, much lower in the sky. The wind had died away, and the air didn't feel as cold. About two hours until dawn, Fargo guessed. And, much closer, Tammy, her heart-shaped face bent over his, her loose russet hair tickling his cheeks.

Still dreaming . . . keep dreaming . . .

Her lips melded with his, parting so their tongues could probe and taste.

Tammy's hand guided his under the blanket wrapping her. She moved it around enough to show him she wasn't wearing a stitch. Then she took his fingers straight to the warm, wet, furry nest between her legs.

"I can't stop thinking' on that big ol' bulge I give you earlier," she cooed as she began moving his hand faster and faster against the slick, chamois-soft lips of her belly mouth. "Just so dang big and thick it was almost scary . . . *nice* scary. Lord, I'm just dripping wet! I need a quick one right now, sugar, 'fore I burn right up."

Fargo, head still filled with sleep fumes, was convinced this must be a dream, but nonetheless had every intention

45

of enjoying it. The slippery broth of her sex quickly soaked his fingers and hand, even beaded warm on his wrist, as she began to buck her hips, rubbing herself quickly to a shuddering, gasping climax.

"There," she said on a sigh. "Now let's *really* get thrashing."

Tammy crawled in with him and undid his trousers. "I got about two dozen of them left in me," she promised him.

She worked his trousers down over his hips, freeing his erection.

"Lordy, Skye!" she marveled, gripping it at the base and stroking him with a velvet touch. "A gal could get muscles churning this big handle."

Tammy pushed his shirt up to rub her pliant, pointy nipples into the curlicues of his chest hair.

He slid his face down and nuzzled his beard against the satiny heft of her breasts. Then he licked, nibbled, sucked, and kissed each nipple even stiffer.

"Oh, you hungry, *hun*-gry animal!" she egged him on.

This is the only way to dream, Fargo congratulated himself as he slid her around on top of him so he could feel that luscious, high-split, polished-ivory behind he'd been thinking about all day. It was firm and shapely, a pleasure to knead each supple-as-angel-food cheek in his hands until she was mewling.

"I promised you I know how to do things to a man," she said in a throaty husk as her head disappeared under the blanket. "But let's give you a quick one first. That way you can work up a long trot for the next one."

"Hon, you *do* know men."

Tammy's hot, wet tongue licked a long and delicious line down his chest, over his stomach, then up the sensitive underside of his aroused manhood. The sudden, intense pleasure made Fargo's legs shudder.

"Oh-ma-*god*!" Tammy marveled. "Honey, you got a *fine* size on you."

She added shyly: "Skye?"

"Hmm?"

"Was that just tease talk earlier to get me all het up— that business 'bout how you like to 'stick your nose in the pie'? See, most fellas won't give a girl that kind of pleasure. I mean . . . see, maybe we could do each other?"

This is my dream, Fargo told himself, and as long as I'm here, I'm gonna have a taste.

"Darlin'," he invited, "just back that sweet fanny around and mount up. I'm one to give as good as I get."

"Well, you're gonna get it *good*, mister, I promise you that."

Tammy straddled his face, then bent forward to take his curved saber into a hungry mouth. She took as much of him as she could, a hot, tight, wet pleasure flowing over his length. Now and then she backed off so just his swollen tip was in her mouth, giving that supersensitive area all the attention of her swirling tongue and talented lips.

As she had promised, her own sex was already hot and ready and juicy-sweet with her love nectar. The moment Fargo's tongue touched her pearl nub she cried out, the sound muffled by his manhood in her mouth.

Gasping, she backed off just long enough to encourage him.

"Oh, sweet, hot *damn* that is nice," she moaned.

Then she plunged him right back into her greedy mouth and began raking her eyeteeth along him with just enough teasing pressure to hurt so nice.

Hot, explosive force was gathering in Fargo's loins, but he willed himself to hold off so he could extend this indescribable erotic pleasure for both of them.

Soon Tammy was firing off climaxes like a string of Chinese firecrackers, as she finally felt Fargo turning steel-hard in her mouth—sure sign of imminent eruption.

The tickling prickle in Fargo's groin swelled to a massive overload demanding release. Moaning simultaneously, they both exploded together in a tangled, writhing confusion of blankets and naked arms and legs.

When her postcoital daze passed and she finally regained awareness, Tammy cuddled her petite body against Fargo and covered them back up against the chill.

"Skye Fargo, you're already hard again!" she exclaimed joyously when she felt his ready organ nudging into her belly. "Well, I ain't *quite* used up my two dozen."

"Waste not, want not," Fargo agreed.

He rolled on top, parted her creamy-soft inner thighs, and fitted himself for a long ride in his favorite saddle.

*　　*　　*

When Fargo woke up, a new sun was rising and he could hear the dawn chorus of birds down in the river growth.

He was alone in his blankets, and a smile divided his beard. Life was odd that way, he thought, a night that began with violence and death could end up sweet as strawberry shortcake.

He kicked off his blankets, straightened his buckskins, shook his boots in case a snake had crawled into one. While he sat down to pull them on, Fargo's lake-blue gaze stayed in motion studying everything. After that killing last night and the humiliating of Jack Duran yesterday, Fargo sensed the trouble was far from over.

In fact, the fandango had just begun. By now Fargo was convinced Tammy and the rest had been lured west by a gang starved of sex. His only real question concerned Mattie and her role in all this.

The ladies might be green, but at least some of them were early risers. Fargo whiffed the tempting odor of coffee and ambled down to their camp.

Mattie, Yvette, and Tammy were up and stirring. He could glimpse the twins still dressing inside the celerity wagon. When they saw him peeking, they blew kisses at him.

Fargo touched his hat as he drew up by the fire. "Morning, ladies. Coffee smells good. I noticed there's a rabbit in my snare. Trade you that for a cup of river mud."

Mattie only ignored him, her features stern as granite. The twins, sleepy-eyed and shy, joined the others. Tammy, looking a little puffy around the eyes but otherwise glowing, handed him a mug of coffee.

"Hope it *tastes* good as it smells," she said with an impish grin. "Sorry there's no pie to go with it."

A sudden wind gust whipped her skirt up. Only then did Fargo spot the grass stains on her knees. He grinned right back.

Yvette greeted him with one of her increasingly bold smiles. "*Bo'jour, M'sieur* Fargo. Sleep well?"

"Sleep!" Mattie butted in. "How could he when he was busy blasting away with firearms and then buried up to his ears in Tammy's petticoats all night! There's your brave 'protector,' girls."

"You was spying!" Tammy accused.

"Spying? You little trollop, you were out there keening like a queen in heat. They heard you back in St. Louis."

"So what? I ain't married yet," Tammy retorted.

"You're promised," Mattie reminded her.

"That's what *you* say."

"That's what a contract says!" Mattie shouted. Again Fargo got the impression she was more desperate and scared than angry.

"That's what you keep saying," Tammy replied. "But I'm starting to think Skye is right. There ain't no Chandlerville nor any Mr. Chandler either."

Mattie smirked. "You *would* agree with him—now he's had his way with you. Or more like it, you had your way with him."

She whirled toward Skye, her eyes blazing. "That's twice yesterday your presence attracted shooting. Why don't you just leave?"

"I aim to," Fargo said, draining his coffee, "just as quick as you tell me where to take you: Fort Walla Walla or Fort Bridger."

Mattie turned so scarlet even her earlobes blushed. "We're going *no*where, and especially not with you."

Unfazed, Fargo stared at her until her show of anger passed and she only looked flustered and helpless.

"I don't have you figured out yet," he told her. "You're obviously playing your cards close. Maybe you've got your reasons. Whatever they are, you think real careful like before you toss these young ladies to the wolves. You hurt them, Mattie, and I don't *care* what your reasons are. You'll answer for it."

He said this mildly. But she paled noticeably and turned away.

Fargo, aiming a complicit wink at Tammy, told her: "I got a little chore to do this morning. If there's any trouble while I'm gone, fire off that musket your pa gave you."

He headed upslope toward his Ovaro, carrying the burlap bag with the would-be killer's head in it. He intended to resume his scout down near the Snake River after meeting later this morning with Snowshoe and Ruck-a-Chucky.

Right now, though, he had a gruesome message to send.

Yvette scampered to catch up with him, and Fargo obligingly shortened his stride.

"What is in the bag, *M'sieur* Fargo?"

"A dead animal," he said, leaving it at that although his reply was an insult to the animal kingdom.

"Skye?" she pressed, switching to his first name. "You know now why we are here in this lonely, desolate place. But why are *you*? A man like you could live like a king in New Orleans."

Fargo knew why, all right, but he couldn't fit words to the feelings. He glanced east, toward the nearest ascending fold of separate mountain ranges that made up the broad Rockies. His eyes rose above the timber palisades to the rock plain; higher yet to the snow line and the blinding-white peaks that never melted. The place where eagles soared free.

There was a clean and stark beauty to this rugged Northwest country. Fargo knew, better than most, just how quickly the pristine West was settling up as history rapidly turned the pages. He'd seen belching smokestacks, five-story hotels, even ice-skating rinks in places he'd once known as empty wilderness.

"It's true this area is harsh and unforgiving," he finally told Yvette as he whistled to the Ovaro. "But I'm hoping a few pockets of the West will always defy human settlement. This place bids fair to become one of 'em."

"Captain Bonneville calls human settlement 'the irrevocable march of civilization.' "

Maybe so, but to Skye Fargo it was a rush to flabby-handed folly. But how do you explain that to a sweet young thing from New Orleans? Her reality came from books and plays, and now she and the other girls were trapped in a place where men killed other human beings as casually as they swatted flies—a place where law and government were fairy-tale notions.

Fargo had learned that lesson all over again last night. And the grisly contents of the burlap bag in his hand bore proof that the bloodletting had only begun.

6

Skye Fargo knew that the hard tails who jumped him last night had enough sense to leave their horses picketed far away and move in on foot. He could waste the entire day trying to find that spot and perhaps cut sign on the lone survivor. So instead he rode straight down to the Snake River and began scouting the east bank, bearing south on a hunch.

Snowshoe had to be right. Since the gang hadn't seized his convenient ferry, they probably had their own fording place in this vicinity, one they hoped would remain their secret. Fargo meant to locate it and then put the contents of his burlap bag to appropriate use.

He kicked the Ovaro up to a fast trot, an energy-saving pace the stallion could hold for hours. Rambling vines that would soon bud with dog roses choked both banks of the river. The whistle of wild plovers and the scolding of angry jays assured him no humans were lurking nearby.

However, he suspected eyes were watching him.

Much of vast Hell's Canyon lay west of the river, a tangled, densely grown expanse crisscrossed by deep glacier scars and swollen, churning creeks. The only "trails" were a few ancient game traces. Despite the area's daunting topography, however, Fargo spotted several hearty prospectors working those creeks with sluice boxes. But who else was taking refuge in that wild place, preying on those sourdoughs and others all over the region?

The stakes here, Fargo reminded himself, were more personal than simply seeing that justice was done. The intended victims now included him and those five so-called contract brides—or at least four of them, depending on

51

Mattie's role. And it was Fargo's style, once he was marked for death, to draw first blood, and plenty of it.

He rounded a dogleg bend in the river and reined in. The Snake narrowed slightly here, forming a bottleneck, and from the opposite bank projected a gravel bar, though he had to squint hard to see it. It had been extended even farther by a line of boulders. Nothing too fancy, and a horse would still have to swim part of the river. But for those very reasons, the spot would draw little attention from any passers-by.

This, Fargo told himself, could be the gang's ford.

He assumed—and even hoped—a distant sentry was watching him through binoculars. But Fargo first made a careful study of the immediate area to make sure no one was notching sights on him. Then he swung down and dropped the bridle so the Ovaro could drink while he knelt to study the riverbank.

His experienced eye quickly sorted out the tracks, mostly old, of beavers, lynx, badgers, otters, muskrats, and raccoons: all smaller animals typical of salt-depleted areas. Except the newest and most unmistakable tracks, two sets of fresh prints where shod horses had crossed the river both ways.

The grass inside the latest set was still slightly bent, suggesting they weren't even a day old yet. The man who had escaped last night had taken his dead partner's mount with him.

Now at least Fargo had a point to start from when he resumed his search for the rats' nest. But that would have to wait until after his meeting later with Ruck-a-Chucky and Snowshoe.

Right now, however, Fargo had an unpleasant but necessary task to perform.

He selected a sapling of the right length, drew the Arkansas Toothpick from his boot to cut it down and trim it, then began sharpening both ends into stakes. While he worked, the rusty sound of a tobacco-roughened singing voice gradually drew nearer.

"Bang-bang Lulu,
Bang 'er ev'ry day,

Who's gonna bang poor Lulu
When I get old and gray?"

A grin parted Fargo's lips. That gravely racket could only
be Snowshoe Hendee, probably riding his traplines along
the river. It was way too early to be showing up with lazy
late-sleeper Ruck-a-Chucky.

But the grin faded when Fargo finished sharpening his
pole at both ends and untied the burlap sack from his cantle strap—riding out earlier, he couldn't bear the thought
of tying it to his saddle horn and feeling it bump his leg
while he rode.

He shook the sack open, and the head rolled out into
the grass like a melon from the market—except that this
melon had two glazed, wide-open eyes staring up at him.

Fargo steeled himself as he pinned the head under his
boot heel and positioned one end of the stake. This was a
distasteful move, and he'd prefer another way to handle
this predicament. But innocent lives were on the line, and
there was no alternative. In the absence of soldiers or law,
there was no choice but to unnerve these parasites and
opportunists.

No one man could kill all of them. So he must try to
make them go puny and slink off in the night like the cowardly vermin they were.

Fargo's jaw muscles bunched tight as he gritted his teeth
and drove the stake deep into the neck-stem of the decapitated head. The off-key bawdy singing was nearer now as
Snowshoe came out of the adjacent bend.

"Lulu had a chicken,
Lulu had a duck,
Put 'em on a table
To see if they would—Augh!"

Snowshoe squeezed his knees to halt Ignatius the mule,
staring in jaw-dropping, wide-eyed astonishment at the
"vengeance pole" his friend was driving into the soft
ground.

"By the two balls of Christ!" Snowshoe exclaimed.
"Well, this child heard the hullabaloo last night, figured
you'd be in the thick of it, Skye."

53

"Snowshoe, how they hangin'?" Fargo greeted his friend, still busy jamming the pole into the ground.

"Feelin' fit as a ruttin' buck," the old salt assured him, sliding nimbly off his mule's swayed back.

He stared up at the ghastly head, now rising about twelve feet into the air. His flint-gray eyes cracked deep at the corners when he grinned and added: "More'n I can say for *that* jack-o'-lantern. 'S'matter, tried to lighten you of your pinto?"

"Tried to bury an ax in my back," Fargo said. "It was dark, his partner tried to put me down with a load from a double-ten. Got his own pal instead."

"A-huh. Good riddance to bad rubbish. But there's talk at the Nez Percé village this morning how three more prospectors was killed and robbed last night, all by white men and all in diggin's scattered far from each other. This gang you're doggin' is big and dug in deep, Skye. Getting shut of them is gonna be harder than snapping snot off a fingernail."

"I think this is one of their fords," Fargo said. "Which is why I planted our friend here. To make sure they get a good look at him. Did you jaw with Chucky?"

Snowshoe nodded. "Says he'll be by later. Prob'ly will; happens he ain't too drunk. He likes you."

"God help me," Fargo muttered. "That red son's shady tricks will sink me yet."

But Snowshoe wasn't really listening. The old trapper stared at the vengeance pole, tugging thoughtfully at his twin-braided beard.

"Skye, you say a double-ten tore this dung heap up last night, uh?"

"Sure's hell sounded like one. Killed him and butchered him out all at the same time."

"A-huh. Hmm . . . 'member when we was both cuttin' sign in Texas? That talk about a killer out west in the Big Bend country, an hombre what packed little Mex'can coins into shotgun shells?"

Fargo nodded. "Sure. The hell was his name? Ludley—Ludman—no, Ludlow. Ace Ludlow. He used to rob express coaches using a female decoy to stop—"

Fargo paused, his own words sinking in. *A female decoy . . .* One like Mattie Everett?

"That's the jasper," Snowshoe said. "Quicksand would spit him back up. Anybody gave him any guff during a heist, he'd blow 'em to smithereens. Rumor has it he lit a shuck for the Northwest after he killed a federal paymaster. Could be him tried to free your soul last night."

"Distinct possibility," Fargo agreed.

And that just might explain Mattie's role in "mother hening" those four beautiful women. She was leading them into a trap.

"Anyhow," Snowshoe said, "this child fears it'll soon be comin' down to the nut-cuttin' around here. The Nez Percés is already on the scrap on accounta all the hair faces trespassing on their rez. And now you're in the mix. Skye Fargo don't just raise hell—he *tilts* it a few feet. You best come with me; I got sumpin' to show you. Might come in handy."

The two men tracked the riverbank north, heading toward Snowshoe's ferry. He had a camp hidden in the thickets beyond it. Besides a crude brush shanty, Fargo noticed a few animal pelts stretched on wooden drying frames.

"I can scrape 'em," Snowshoe explained as they dismounted. "But I can't soften nor tan 'em till I lay in some more salt. Don't matter no how, that-'ere's a month's work—six goldang pelts! The Injins got one thing right, anyhow. It's settlement and farming what destroys the fur-bearing animals."

Fargo instinctively sympathized with the bitter edge in Snowshoe's tone. Most folks considered land worthless if it wasn't inhabited and put to profitable use. Men like Fargo and Snowshoe saw it just the opposite. Too often, the value of a place went down as settlers moved in.

"Ahh, t'hell with it, the snows of yesteryear and all that truck," Snowshoe opined gruffly. "I didn't fetch you here to bellyache about the stingy trappin'. Follow me, hoss, you need to see this."

Snowshoe had used a hatchet to clear a narrow passage through some tangled thickets. It led to a backwater of the Snake.

"There," Snowshoe announced. "Case you ever have need of it."

Fargo stared at a large wooden river skiff. It was the type

favored by explorers and traders, capable of transporting a sizable cargo. A small swivel-mounted cannon, about thirty inches in length, projected from the bow.

"That skiff's clinker-built and good work," Snowshoe said. "Looks like the work of French Canadians. Figure they had to make a portage over land and cached it, then never come back. Anyhow, I sealed her with pine pitch, and she's waterproof as a bullfrog."

"That's a big bow gun for a skiff," Fargo remarked. "Matter fact, it's more a keelboat weapon. Usually you'll see a blunderbuss on a skiff. That cannon a one-pounder?"

Snowshoe spat amber, then nodded and grinned wickedly. "A-huh. And there's no loads for it. But she takes a nice handful of rifle or musket balls. Cuts a wider swath that way, too—happens you take my drift?"

Fargo matched the old coot's grin, recalling Tammy's leather pouch filled with deadly one-ounce musket balls. Sixteen of them would pack neatly into that cannon. Fargo had once seen such a load obliterate half the crew of a flatboat on the Missouri River.

"That cannon's easy to unhook," Snowshoe added. "Two men could lug 'er easy. Put a delay fuse in that touchhole, you got you a bomb. You possess a devious mind, Skye, when it comes to fighting a rough set-to. And no matter how you slice it, the fight's here. That vengeance pole you set up *will* ruffle some feathers and bring lead flyin'."

Fargo nodded. "It's meant to. The message is clear: Fill your hand or clear out."

As if to remind him of that very message, Fargo again caught a scent of wood smoke. The breeze was from the southwest—and the heart of rugged Hell's Canyon.

"This child smells it, too," Snowshoe said, watching his friend's nose sample the air.

"Ride back with me to my camp," Fargo said, heading back toward his horse. "Should be a few hours yet before Chucky shows up. You keep an eye on those gals. I'm gonna cross the river at that ford and make a quick scout, see if that smoke leads me anywhere interesting."

Ace Ludlow was getting mighty damn worried.

About thirty minutes earlier one of the sentries, so agitated he was stuttering, had reported that Fatty McGratten's head was staked near the gang's nearest river ford, vultures already circling. Now, all the men were awake, and rage, frustration, anger, and the first trace of fear all lingered like a thick odor in the close air of the cabin.

"So he's already located our ford," Ace fretted. "I *told* you dumb bastards not to cook during the day. Hell, why not run up a pirate's flag while you're at it?"

But the sullen faces surrounding him scared Ace out of his tantrum in a hurry. It didn't matter that gold dust and nuggets were piling up under the floor planks. Not only were the living conditions miserable, now there was danger in the mix. Fatty McGratten had been a feared and respected killer. Yet this meddling stranger had just finished feeding Fatty's head to the carrion birds. And obviously he was closing in on their hideout, the key to their survival.

"Ace, you sure you can trust that damn woman of yours?" Hoyt Jackson demanded. "The longer this bastard is around her, the bigger the chance she'll spill the beans."

Hoyt was playing draw poker with three other men. The stakes, in lieu of cash, were wolf scalps and strings of coyote feet—always good for bounty at various county seats throughout the settled West. Other bored men scattered around the cabin, awaiting orders, were playing dominoes and checkers.

"Don't sweat none about Mattie," Ace assured his lackey. "When I say hawk, that gal spits. One letter from me to the Governor of Texas, and she'll be in one a them women's prisons with horse-faced matrons that *hate* pretty gals."

Mattie did indeed fear Ace, he was sure of it. But he also knew women were notional creatures—and Mattie still a damn fine-looking woman at thirty. If that crusader touched her, Ace swore to kill both of them. *No* son of a bitch ate off Ace Ludlow's plate.

Hoyt smacked his discards down so hard he shook the heavy table.

"Don't piss down our backs and tell us it's raining, Ace! You swore up and down them hoors'd be spreading their legs in the sportin' parlor by now. But here we all are, still 'holding our own,' *if* you take my drift?"

An echoing rumble of complaints swept through the cabin. Ace was about to reply when a trapdoor in the floor banged open and Jack Duran climbed up from the secret tunnel. Its entrance was hidden in a cut bank down near the west bank of the Snake. Such secret "Indian tunnels" were common on the frontier for emergency escapes. This one was even handier because it allowed the shack to be virtually overgrown by surrounding brush while also eliminating telltale trails.

Duran had just returned from viewing Fatty's head for himself. He propped his Big Fifty against a wall and stared around the cabin at all the expectant faces. His mean little terrier face was even more pinched with smoldering rage.

"His eyes was wide open. Staring out at me like them glass gewgaws they use for eyes in them dolls for little girls. I cannot abide a staring corpse."

"Corpse?" Hoyt snorted. "Hell, all that's left is a damn head. What did that son of a bitch *do* to Fatty, Ace?"

"Best I could tell in the confusion, he tricked Fatty with a decoy and then back-shot him. I damn near burned him, but he got behind a stone windbreak in the nick of time. I s'poze he figures mutilating the body will put snow in our boots."

Ace was almost certain he himself had torn Fatty asunder with his field howitzer. He had taken a wild chance on killing the other man, and figured Fatty was expendable. However, he wasn't stupid enough to admit that. Let the others think the stranger decapitated Fatty. That should motivate them to kill him quicker.

Motivate some of them, he corrected himself. A few others looked a little pale and uncertain.

One of those men who had just joined the gang, a former muleteer from Kansas named Zeke Barlow, now spoke up.

"Judging on what you fellers've said, I'm thinking I know who this hombre is. Skye Fargo. Some call him the Trailsman."

"Katy Christ!" exclaimed one of the card players. "Fargo? I hear he's a good man to let alone."

Zeke Barlow nodded. "Matter fact, 'counta him I damn near lost my hair in the Black Hills out in Dakota. We had a sweet little gold operation humming along until he helped the Sioux drive us out."

"Now hold on, boys," Ace cut in. "All right, so Fatty

was some pumpkins with an ax. But face it. He never was the brightest spark in the campfire. He was mule-kicked in the head when he was just a tadpole. Him gettin' killed ain't no reason to choke."

Zeke said, "But this Trailsman's reputation—"

"T'hell with his reputation," Ace snarled. "The only reason that whoreson ain't feeding worms right now, and them women ain't got their ankles behind their ears for us, is the need to protect this hideout. He *will* die, and damn soon. The sentries have orders to shoot him on sight."

Hoyt scowled. "That's fine if he comes around quick, but what if he don't? I say let's go take what's ours."

"I told you before, Hoyt, we can't risk just riding up in a blazing show of force. In broad daylight, kill him, grab screaming women, and hightail it back here? We make too much noise and tip the local vigilantes off about where we are. . . . Well, I don't need to spell it out, do I? They'll use our guts for tether reins."

"You got one thing right, Ace," Jack Duran said. "Skye Fargo, or whoever the hell he is, *will* die damn soon—and damn hard, mark my words. But you and Fatty messed it up good. Now, by eternal thunder, *I* get the next crack at him."

While he spoke, Duran was stropping his cutthroat razor on a strip of flexible leather, one end of which was nailed to the deal table.

He held the razor up so the others could see the honed blade glint cruelly in the light of a kerosene lamp.

"Boys, this li'l honey is Toledo steel. Cuts so fine I can curl off just the thin outer skin, until a man's all raw and exposed. Then you stake him out on top an anthill and watch the circus begin. You ain't *heard* screaming till you hear a peeled man being chewed for hours by red ants."

One of the new men was standing behind Duran's chair. He grinned and then tapped his right temple. *Room for rent*, the gesture said.

But absolutely no one smiled or laughed. Least of all Ace or Hoyt, who knew Duran best. He was unstable niter, and nobody was foolish enough to shake him. The cabin went silent except for the steady, spine-tickling sound of steel scraping leather.

"Yessir," Duran said, "*let* Mister Skye Goddamn Fargo enjoy our women. I plan to settle accounts with that mange pot."

Feeding vultures flapped reluctantly away from the spiked head, scrawking angrily, when Fargo returned to the natural ford.

The Snake was bank full and running briskly, but with the gravel bar and bridge of boulders extending from the opposite bank, it would be a short swim.

Fargo swung down and loosened the girth so the Ovaro could swim stronger and hold his breath longer in case of trouble. The fearless stallion plunged right in, and Fargo immediately let himself slide back over the cantle and into the ice-cold river, holding his pinto's tail like a towrope.

They were across and climbing onto shore in less than a minute. Fargo was cinching the girth tight again when a fist-sized chunk of bark suddenly flew off the tree beside him. A split-second later the loud whip-crack of a high-caliber rifle shattered the stillness as the sound caught up with the bullet.

Instantly, Fargo's trail experience read the clues. That gap between impact and sound was large enough to imply a very long-distance shot, meaning that the first bullet was almost certainly just a ranging shot so the hidden marksman could adjust his sights or his aim.

Which meant the next shot would be for score.

Fargo read all this even as he sprang into action. The Ovaro had reared up at the shot. Fargo, holding the bridle reins, slapped his stallion hard on its glossy rump to jump it forward. Together they crashed straight ahead into the dense river thickets. The Ovaro's size and weight served as a sort of rolling crusher, trampling down brush and clearing them a safe spot.

Sheltered now, Fargo quickly dried off his weapons, then pulled the brass-framed Army binoculars from a saddlebag. He spent a long time in those thickets, patiently studying as much as Hell's Canyon as he could see from his vantage point.

Fargo worked systematically, dividing the terrain into sectors and studying each one minutely. And finally his patient vigilance paid off—he glimpsed a lean, hard face that seemed carved out of bone.

It belong to a man—make that a sentry, Fargo told himself—perched on the limb of a spreading oak tree about three hundred yards northwest of the ford. He was craning his neck, no doubt looking for Fargo.

"Well, old son," Fargo muttered as he levered a round into the chamber of his Henry, " 'pears I owe you a bullet."

He took up a sitting-offhand position. With his thumb he smeared the glare off his front sight. His sights were set for game—about two hundred yards—so he raised the muzzle slightly to allow for bullet drift.

Fargo breathed deeply and relaxed completely as he aimed and took up the trigger slack, squeezing ever so steadily to avoid bucking the weapon.

The Henry kicked into his shoulder, blood plumed from the sentry's chest, and he fell crashing from the tree, snapping off branches as he plummeted.

"Kill one fly," Fargo told his horse, "kill a million."

He had hoped to detect the scent of wood smoke again and trace it to its source. But Fargo noticed nothing now. He checked the slant of the sun and decided it would soon be time to meet with Ruck-a-Chucky, assuming he showed up.

But Fargo would be back down here—and soon. That now dead sentry was proof he was getting close to the gang's hideout. And where there was smoke, there was always fire.

7

"Skye Fargo, you sheep-humping son of Satan!" Snowshoe Hendee fumed when Fargo returned to the twin camps on the mountain slope. "Protect the women? By the Lord Harry, they damn near kilt *me*, boy!"

Snowshoe pointed downslope toward the women's camp.

"You never said them gals is loaded for bear. That-'ere little piece with the cinnamon braid," he said, meaning Tammy, "took after me with a musket longer 'n she is. And that gal what looks to be the oldest, why, she braced me with a goldang Colt Navy. This child would be a gone beaver right now happens he hadn't blurted out your name."

Fargo grinned as he swung down and stripped the tack from his horse. The Ovaro hadn't even broken a sweat in this brisk weather, so Fargo just turned him out to graze without rubbing him down.

"Hell, so what?" he replied. "A bullet would just ricochet off that old leather hide of yours anyhow."

Snowshoe grinned and spat amber. "Reckon that rings right. Ol' Snowshoe's been shot, stabbed, speared, pierced by arrahs, clawed by grizz, and had so many broken bones knit crooked he can tell you when a twister's comin'. Speaking of shots . . . I heerd two from the river while you was gone."

Fargo nodded. "Some jay perched in a tree tried to knock me out from under my hat."

"And now they's one less jay in the tree, uh?"

"True, but plenty more at the nest, I'd wager."

"A-huh. Like maggots in moldy meat."

Snowshoe cheeked his cud, then scowled and added, "It

makes me ireful! By-god men like Kit Carson and Jim Bridger and Dan'l Boone took a few Injin game traces and turned 'em into wagon roads. But for what? A flood of murderin' thieves, that's what. And a passel of soft-handed, dough-bellied boardwalkers what can't tell a pommel from a cantle. I snore, they'd all starve and go naked without stores."

"We're both fossils," Fargo agreed. "But no need to work yourself into a fit over it, Snowshoe. You lived your prime right smack in the shining times. And you follow the old ways still. We can't stop what's coming, but we can drink life to the lees now. Quit whining and look down there."

Snowshoe's scowl faded as his eyes followed Fargo's finger and gazed downslope. Tammy, Yvette, and the Papenhagen twins were all doing laundry at the little runoff stream. Tammy waved up toward them.

Snowshoe chuckled. "Washin' out their dainties right in front of us. Saucy little tarts. You been a-pokin' that little filly with the cinnamon braid, aintcher? Lookit how she's primping around for you. Why'n't you get *me* a little bit o' that stuff, hoss? Mebbe one a them-'ere blondes?"

"You?" Fargo, who had squatted on his heels beside the ashes of a fire Snowshoe made earlier, ran a wiping patch through the bore of his Henry. "Hell, Methuselah, I only meant for you to look. Any one of those gals would leave you dead in bed, you old goat."

"Oh, *my* snake still bites. C'mon . . . le'me slip into your bedroll after dark, they won't know. Hell, we both got beards and peckers, ain't we? A nod's as good as a wink to a blind mule."

"Yeah, but even a blind mule has still got a nose," Fargo reminded him. "You smell like a tub of ripe guts, old codger."

"Ahh, go piss up a rope. Bathing is for women and squaw men."

Snowshoe was still staring down toward the women. "Yessir, this child *does* admire a fine set of catheads on a wench. Look-a-here, Skye."

Snowshoe, who sat cross-legged in the grass, handed Fargo his rifle. It was a typical Plains rifle from the celebrated Hawken shop in St. Louis. A 34-inch octagonal barrel, .53 caliber, with a sturdy, crescent-shaped butt plate that fit neatly into the shoulder. It fired half-ounce round balls.

But it wasn't the weapon itself Snowshoe meant. It was the beautiful naked dancer carved and painted on one side of the half stock.

"That-'ere's the Whore of Babylon," Snowshoe said proudly. "Like them titties? The artwork was done personal like for me by Mr. Nathan Jones of Raccoon Creek, Kentucky. Lookit there how the nipples is little chips of ruby, hey?"

Lovingly, Snowshoe traced the ruby nubbins with the tip of his index finger. "Me, I'm the boy for a *fine* set of tits."

"I prefer the kind that respond when they're touched," Fargo replied from a deadpan. "Jesus, maybe we had better get you a live woman."

A few seconds later he added, "Say . . . ain't that Ruck-a-Chucky riding up from the river?"

A stout horsebacker in a warm sheepskin coat had just emerged from the thick growth near the Snake. In Fargo's experience most Indian ponies were pintos, usually piebald or skewbald. But this region also featured the famous Appaloosas, beautiful saddle horses with spotted rumps, bred by the Nez Percés.

"Yup, that's Chucky," Snowshoe confirmed. "That-'ere 'loosa is part of his farce that he's a Nez Percé chief. See how he's teetering in the saddle. He's all jollified from whiskey."

Fargo shook his head in amazement at the audacious Indian grifter. Ruck-a-Chucky had indeed married a Nez Percé woman. But he himself was a California Modoc with some Palouse blood. However, the California and Northwest tribes were numerous and confusing to outsiders. And Ruck-a-Chucky's odd but solid skill in speaking English put him in an excellent position to work schemes involving whites.

Snowshoe snorted. "Can you b'lieve some damn fool Mormon told me the American Indians're part of the Ten Lost Tribes of Israel? That-'ere red son is lost, all right— lost in a fog of lazy schemes and rotgut fumes. He's like a little kid, know that, Skye? He don't mean no harm. But he's a greedy-guts. When he sniffs profit, he points like a hound dog."

Fargo said, "I'll grant you he don't mean no harm. But neither does an avalanche, yet the damn thing'll kill you just as dead."

"A-huh," Snowshoe agreed. "I like the son of a buck. He's true-blue with his friends. But that-'ere's a dangersome Injin."

Ruck-a-Chucky was well up the slope now, close enough that Fargo heard the faint clinking of his Appaloosa's bit chain. Mattie hurried toward the celerity wagon. Probably to get her gun, Fargo mused, wondering if he was making a mistake to let Mattie keep it. Then again, he didn't like the idea of seizing anyone's weapon before he had proof against her. This was the wild frontier, not the Land of Steady Habits back East.

"It's all right, ladies!" Fargo shouted down toward them. "You won't need weapons. He's friendly and harmless. I sent for him."

Ruck-a-Chucky was almost on them now, his face wreathed in a grin. He was unequivocally homely, a huge and sloppy ragbag of a man with big pouches like bruises under his eyes. His long black hair reeked of bear fat and was held back out of his eyes by a leather cord.

But his silly, high-falsetto giggle and boy-howdy enthusiasm were infectious. Already giggling uncontrollably as he rode up, he half-fell, half-jumped from his horse and clasped Fargo in a bear hug, lifting him off the ground.

"Well, for corn sakes, it's Skye Fargo!" he exclaimed in a perfect imitation of a Southern drawl.

Fargo and Snowshoe exchanged a grin. Ruck-a-Chucky possessed an extraordinary trait by birth: He was "echoic" like a parrot, only quicker to learn. He could repeat sounds perfectly even without knowing their meaning, so they never knew what might fly out of his mouth, or in what dialect.

Under his sheepskin coat Ruck-a-Chucky wore a long and filthy frock coat and blue cavalry trousers with yellow piping on the legs. Fargo noticed a bow and quiver lashed to his horse. The quiver held a few pitifully crooked arrows cut from ash saplings. The sinew bowstring looked frayed and loose. All for show. But Ruck-a-Chucky was a fair hand with the Smith & Wesson repeating rifle in his saddle boot.

"Here's to dark bars and fair women," the Indian quoted some frontier wag as he tipped back his bottle.

"Chucky," Fargo greeted him, "you are one raggedy-assed excuse of an Indian. But I like you, you drunken sot."

Ruck-a-Chucky loosed a string of giggles, then nodded vigorously.

"Ja, dot iss true, py golly!" he replied.

Hearing this one, Snowshoe laughed so hard he had a coughing fit and leaked tobacco juice all over his braided beard and doeskin shirt. That set Ruck-a-Chucky off on another attack of giggles. Fargo, who had meant to take the errant Modoc harshly to task, burst into laughter himself. Even all five women, watching from below, had caught the giggles.

"Now damnit, Chucky," Fargo said when he could look stern again, "this is serious. What's this I hear about you masquerading as a Nez Percé chief?"

"Lies."

"Yeah? Then how come you got your nose rigged up like that?"

Fargo meant the piece of white shell Ruck-a-Chucky wore dangling from his septum. It was this custom that inspired the French name Nez Percés or "pierced noses." Except that Ruck-a-Chucky's was cleverly faked, not actually piercing the septum.

"My wife—"

"She's nothing to the matter. *You* are mostly Modoc. And you're a long way from your tribal area. Is it true you've been selling prospectors 'contracts' so they can pan gold on the Nez Percé reservation?"

Ruck-a-Chucky stuffed a clay pipe with black shag. He rolled an ember out of that morning's fire with the toe of his triple-soled moccasin. Picking it up between two stones, he fired his pipe. He simply ignored Fargo's question.

"Chucky," Fargo persisted, "are you a bigger fool than God made you? Not only are the Nez Percés going to flay your soles, but you're luring white fools to their death. The Nez Percés tend to like whites, and *may*be they'll just drive them out. But the bad element you've also lured isn't so considerate."

Ruck-a-Chucky wasn't giggling now. Skye Fargo had once saved his bacon, and the Modoc did value his good opinion of him. And clearly Fargo was angry. Chucky's moon face looked contrite.

But Fargo wasn't fooled. One major goal of the Lewis and Clark expedition had been to convince these Far West Indians they owed allegiance to a new, unknown power. But as Ruck-a-Chucky proved, it would be easier to put socks on a rooster than to "nationalize" an Indian. Nor could Fargo blame them—he himself rode under no colors.

"It is not as you hear it, Fargo," Ruck-a-Chucky said. The drawl was back when he added, "Not on your tin-type, mister!"

He swept one arm out widely, indicating Hell's Canyon. From this elevation, and with the slant of the late-morning sun, several of the glittering, gold-rich creeks could be seen.

"My contracts, they allow the gold-seekers *only* into a few areas the Nez Percé tribe do not use or even visit. But it was like a grass fire. The whites have quickly spread past my boundaries. Even without the contracts they would do the same."

Fargo had to concede that point. Before Ruck-a-Chucky ever got into the mix, steamboats were lugging their way up the Columbia River into the Snake. They docked at Lewiston, and the prospectors immediately spread right across a favorite Nez Percé campground. So far, the Nez Percés, distracted by intertribal wars, had not reacted.

"Well, are you at least going to stop?" Fargo demanded. "Hell, Chucky, if you're so set on being a rich man, why not earn your fortune the honest way? I've got some money left from a railroad-guard job back in Wyoming Territory. I'll grubstake you. The Comstock Lode isn't played out yet."

When Ruck-a-Chucky frowned at this idea, Fargo demanded, "Why not? You too damn lazy to work?"

Snowshoe grunted. "Would a cow lick Lot's wife? Chucky's strong as horse radish, but he's a lazy cuss."

Ruck-a-Chucky giggled and nodded. "You bet your bucket!"

"Chucky," Fargo persisted, "you *owe* me. Have you forgotten about that lynch mob in the High Sierra?"

Reluctantly, the Modoc shook his head. "Skye is Chucky's friend, you bet. No more contracts."

"Good man. Maybe you can help me another way."

Fargo explained the situation with the women and the clear signs that the gang of killers and thieves plaguing the entire region was located near here.

"You know this area good," Fargo said. "Seen anything in the way of a possible hideout? This would be west of the Snake in Hell's Canyon."

"Chucky has seen nothing," he said. "It is wild and thickly grown, with few trails. That place is Wendigo, best to stay away. But I spoke with a Pelloat Pallah who knows this area."

Ruck-a-Chucky used the old name the explorers gave to the tribe now called Palouse.

"He told me a strange thing. He swears there is a spot near here, a cut bank beside the Snake, where he saw the earth swallow a white man and his horse."

"Swallow?" Fargo repeated. "What—maybe a cave?"

Ruck-a-Chucky, busy stirring his pipe with a twig, only shrugged one huge shoulder.

"Near bank or far?" Fargo asked.

"Far."

Fargo nodded thoughtfully. " 'Preciate the help, Chucky. And you promise—straight arrow—to stop selling them damn contracts?"

Ruck-a-Chucky scowled. "Straight arrow," he finally promised.

"A-huh. Straight like the ones in your quiver," Snowshoe quipped.

Irritated that he had to lose profits, the Modoc was suddenly on his dignity.

"Chucky likes Skye Fargo. But the whiteskins are liars. The white chief in the place beyond the Great Water claims he wants the red man to prosper with the white. More lies."

Fargo shrugged. "Hell, where's the scrap? We're all a bunch of liars. White man lies to the red man, red man lies to the white, I lie to every woman who asks me if her ass is fat."

Ruck-a-Chucky, who held a grudge about as long as he might hold an honest job, snorted at this.

"My woman?" he retorted, cupping both hands in front of his chest. "Flat as a beaver's tail. If I tell her the truth she will cut me bad. She is good with the knife. And she has a strange interest in the white man's practice of gelding stallions."

At these last words, Snowshoe and Fargo exchanged a long glance, the mirth bleeding from their faces. Both men shifted uncomfortably, unconsciously adjusting their trousers.

"You know, *Chief*," Snowshoe remarked from a scowling face, "you don't have to speak *every* damn thought that pops into your head."

By the time Ruck-a-Chucky had left to return to his camp several miles upriver, the sun was almost straight overhead.

"What's on the spit?" Snowshoe asked his friend. "By now the gang knows you've killed that sentry. That makes two you've sent under. You ain't their favorite boy right now, Skye. They could come at any time, in force, hell-bent for leather."

"But they haven't," Fargo pointed out. "That tells me they're not stupid. They know there's a vigilante bunch looking for them. Why else would they sneak up on me at night, try to kill me with an ax 'stead of a gun? Because they're scared of revealing their camp."

"That rings right," Snowshoe said. "But happens you're right 'bout them gals? That means you got the gang's cottontails, and it's so close now they can sniff it. *Every* man turns stupid when his codpiece drains off his brain blood. They won't hold their powder forever, boy."

"No," Fargo agreed. "Which means I can't wait on them to keep calling the tunes—I need to put *them* on the defensive, keep rattling their nerves. Tell me, how many folks use that ferry of yours?"

Snowshoe frowned and dug at something in his left armpit. "Ain't had nary customer yet."

"Then it won't cost you any money if you stay around here for a while, right, keep an eye on the women? Maybe two, three days? I need to take another squint around by the river, see if there's anything to this story of Chucky's about a place that 'swallows men.' "

Snowshoe glanced downslope. The Papenhagen twins were draping their freshly washed pantalets and chemises over tree limbs to dry them in the sun and breeze.

"Might get a little bit o' sugar tit," the old lecher speculated. "Hell, yes, this child will nest on them chicks while you're out seeing if you can get yourself kilt."

"They'll eat you alive, old man."

Snowshoe winked. "A-huh. That means they'll be havin' a ball, don't it?"

Fargo grinned as he slid the newly cleaned and oiled Henry back into the saddle boot. Then he scooped up his bridle and saddle and headed out toward the grazing Ovaro.

"Watch your back trail!" Snowshoe shouted behind him. "Ace Ludlow could be in the mix. That son of a bitch is so low he could walk under a snake's belly on stilts. You already seen what that-'ere scattergun o' his can do. Keep your eyes to all sides, boy, and your nose in the wind."

8

By now, Fargo assumed, he was under constant observation from the tangled depths of Hell's Canyon anytime he rode the open slopes overlooking his side of the Snake. So he moved quickly into the screening timber and dense brush beside the river. It was difficult and slow traveling, but safer.

He never even considered turning south and returning to the gang's ford. Fargo needed to cross the river and get onto the far bank unobserved. Only then could he conduct a search near the river.

That meant bearing north to Snowshoe's unused ferry. Fargo figured it was probably beyond the gang's usual sentry lines, or they'd have seized or destroyed it by now.

With no trail to follow it was slow going anyway. So he gave the Ovaro his head, not worrying when the stallion paused now and then to graze a tempting bunch of new grass or nibble a tender shoot. Fargo liked to move slowly and sporadically in close, hostile terrain, trusting to the natural instincts of his horse. It was rapid or steady motion that generally invited an enemy's bullets.

They reached Snowshoe's twin-dugout ferry without incident. The sturdy, hollowed-out cottonwood logs easily held the nervous but cooperative Ovaro as Fargo pulled them both across by the guide rope, muscles steeled to fight the tug of a brisk current.

Despite the fact that much of the river growth would not bud into leaf for weeks yet, thick stands of juniper and scrub pine provided good cover on this bank. Fargo sought out the low-lying bottomland that forms near most rivers.

Then he turned back toward the south and the more re-mote depths of Hell's Canyon.

He knew his work was cut out for him. If there really was some kind of cave or tunnel, it had to be secluded and well-hidden. That was an especially tall order when horses were included.

The sun was westering by now. Its slant told Fargo when an hour had passed, then two. He gnawed on a strip of jerked buffalo and patiently studied the ground they covered.

He knew he was back into the dangerous sector covered by the gang's sentries. Fargo sought out low seams. At places where the ground leveled out, he led his horse by the bridle reins to lower their skyline.

Finally, his patient vigilance paid off.

He had reached a spot where the river, which had been about fifty feet to his left, now made one of the abrupt, twisting bends for which the Snake was named. This sudden shift placed Fargo abruptly at the edge of the river, nearly exposed.

He wanted the bottom stretch again, and turned right. Just then, however, Fargo's trail-honed hearing detected a muffled sound above the whooshing roar of the river—the sound of several men's coarse laughter, as if at the punch line of a joke.

Oddly, the ever-alert Ovaro had still caught no man scent. Fargo instantly dismounted, for he had no idea where the men were except that they sounded fairly close. He encircled the Ovaro's neck with both arms and, speaking low into the stallion's ear, tugged it toward the ground.

Horses seldom lay down except when sick or for a quick roll. But the Ovaro was trained to lie flat on its side at Fargo's command—a move that had saved them more than once in shooting scrapes on the open plains. Fargo wanted the big pinto out of sight until he located those voices.

Low-crawling slowly and carefully to a spot near the bend, Fargo peeked through a spidery maze of brambles.

At first he saw nothing unusual. The sudden, sharp twist in the river had worn away the bank, forming a shallow cut bank like hundreds along the Snake. But the voices sounded closer now, and Fargo's slitted gaze noticed something—the cut bank only appeared shallow at first glance.

In fact, a chamber (probably natural at first, then widened by men) opened off at right angles from the rear of the cut bank.

Fargo had no plan and couldn't form one until he had a better look at the location and the men. Nor could he see any point in delaying. He meant what he had told Snowshoe about waging this battle on *his* schedule and terms, not the enemy's.

Fargo slid the riding thong from the hammer of his Colt and loosened his Arkansas Toothpick in its boot sheath. Then he placed his hat on the ground, pressed himself flat against the topsoil, and began inching closer along the bank of the frothing river.

"All that juicy stuff sittin' *just* close enough to tease us," Hoyt Jackson complained bitterly. "And Ace actin' like a goddamn weak sister. That's what got Fatty, and now Ulrick, killed. Know that, boys?"

Hoyt, Jack Duran, and one of the new men, Zeke Barlow, were having a smoke in the hidden, makeshift corral they themselves had helped widen with shovels.

Partly underground, partly open, it was invisible from the bank when the horses were kept tightly bunched at the same end where the tunnel emerged, and nearly invisible from the river. The narrow tunnel, reinforced with timber beams like a mine shaft, ran about one hundred yards to the completely overgrown cabin.

"Come down off your hind legs," Duran told Hoyt. "It's this crusading asshole Skye Fargo who killed Fatty and Ulrick, not Ace. And I mean to put his fire out permanent. He made a big mistake when he gelded me in front of them women. Ain't *no* son of a bitch talks down to me like he done."

Hoyt's swarthy face twisted into an angry scowl. "T'hell with your personal grudge. Who cares who kills him so long as the bastard dies? All this damn pussyfootin' around like a buncha Digger Indians stealing a farmer's cow. I want quiff, and damnitall, I want it *now*."

Duran took a last drag off his butt and flicked it away in an arc. "I know, Hoyt, I know. But Ace has got a point about keeping our location secret. Otherwise we're up shit creek. Don't fret, we'll get our women. I'd guess by tomorrow for sure. This Fargo is too stupid to clear out. So, hey? He's al-*ready* dead."

"Balls," Hoyt retorted. "Ace is—"

"Psst!" Zeke Barlow hissed. "I hear somebody in the tunnel."

A few moments later Ace Ludlow emerged, squinting in the bright sunlight. His "field howitzer" lay across the crook of his elbow. His hard-bitten stare shifted from man to man.

"The hell, boys?" he demanded. "This a goddamn tea party? Only Zeke's s'poze to be on guard out here. Look how my horse's ass is sticking out into open view from above! Jack, I thought you and Hoyt was out dogging Fargo?"

"I'd say it's Fargo dogging us," Hoyt gainsaid. "First Fatty, now Linton Ulrick's shot off his tree limb. Zeke's been telling us stories about this Trailsman, boss. Sounds like he's one who knows how to cut up rough. We can't just let him keep playing shoot-at-rovers with us. He'll pick us off like ducks on a fence."

Ace's hard, tight-lipped smile was straight as a seam, and mirthless. "Now there you're right, Hoyt. *If* we let him. But we won't."

"Pick us off, my lily-white ass," Duran scoffed. "Fargo ain't got enough hard in him to kill Jack Duran. Fatty and Ulrick just got careless is all."

"Don't sell him short," Ace cautioned Jack. "Down in the Texas brush country, we got *ladinos*. Wild, killer longhorns that hide in the brush and attack men. Crafty, cunning sons of bitches just like Fargo, if that's his true moniker."

"A crafty and cunning killer, huh? Well, that's *me* you just described," Duran boasted.

He placed a hand on his sheathed razor. "And I nurse a grudge until it hollers mama. I mean to peel off that bastard's skin and let the red ants feast on him."

Ace nodded encouragement. "See there, Hoyt? Jack's got the right spirit. Never mind Zeke's tales. That's all they are—tales. Sure, this Fargo is a hard case. But he puts his pants on one leg at a time like every man. And he *bleeds* like every man. We got too much at stake here to go puny because of one crusader."

Ace had seen firsthand, growing up in the violent Rio Grande country, how the contraband trade spawned powerful criminal gangs. They controlled entire regions with almost no interference from starmen or soldiers, who were scarce, underpaid, and thus usually easy to bribe.

This region, too, was ripe for a far-flung criminal empire. And it, too, included an international border just to the north. Ace would use the stolen gold to get his empire started. By the time the color played out, he meant to become the region's contraband king. Smuggling was safer than killing men in their bedrolls—vigilantes didn't drag-hang smugglers or even worry about them.

But Ace was a practical man. He knew all his big plans were mere mental vapors if his brutal and dangerous men rebelled. Which they soon would if those comely lasses were not flat on their backs in the sporting parlor, and mighty damn quick.

Time to toss the dogs a bone, he realized.

"Boys," he said, putting swagger into his tone, "don't worry overmuch about Skye Fargo. We *will* settle his hash, and quick. Jack here ain't one to make a brag he don't back up. But don't forget—there's also my woman, Mattie."

"She'd kill Fargo?" Hoyt asked, his tone dubious.

Ace's self-satisfied manner was back in spades. "She's got a Colt Navy I gave her, and I taught her how to use it."

"All right. You're saying she *could* kill him," Hoyt said. "But will she? You don't make her out to be a killer. Just a sharper."

"She will if I tell her. Mattie does *any* damn thing I tell her," Ace boasted. "And just maybe having her kill Fargo can be arranged. That's Mattie's specialty—playing horny men for suckers."

Inch by slow inch, Fargo had improved his position. He literally clung to the very lip of the bank, in danger of tumbling into the river. But now he could see more than he could standing up at ground level.

The roaring river was too close, and Fargo couldn't hear what the four men were actually saying. But his line of sight was much better now. Besides the claybank gelding, he could see Jack Duran's big sorrel and several other horses. There was a big wooden rain barrel, even a wooden grain trough so they wouldn't need to openly graze their mounts. He saw one end of a crude hitching post.

Hidden only partially by the bank and a clump of sparse brush, Fargo studied the four men. He instantly recognized Duran's mean, pinched features. The other three were strangers, though their general type was all too familiar to Fargo. Surly, murdering louts who spent their usually brief lives wreaking havoc and pain on the innocent.

But his eyes dwelled longer on one of them: leather *chivarra* trousers, a rawhide vest, a red bandanna, fancy spurs of Mexican silver.

Texan Ace Ludlow, he guessed. And that must be the infamous coin-loaded scattergun he was toting. The same one that tore Ludlow's skinny partner into shreds last night.

Fargo had seen the all-too-familiar scene before, but it still sent a bitter bile taste into his throat. Anywhere opportunity sprouted up, these parasites rapidly moved in. He had watched these predatory outside gangs penetrate all the way west to the Yosemite, the San Joaquin Valley, even into the Sierra Nevada.

And now here in the heart of the Northwest. New devils for ancient Hell's Canyon.

Fargo had no intention of making a play now. Not against four heavily armed men in broad daylight while his ass was dangling over the river. But at least now he knew where the rat's nest was located—well, the no-longer-secret entrance to it, at least. The situation was now his to control—or botch.

Something suddenly moved across the back of Fargo's calves, and he stiffened, then instantly relaxed and lay still as death, knowing what it was.

But that momentary tensing had alerted the rattlesnake now slithering over his legs. Fargo heard the sudden, menacing buzz of its rattle.

He knew he was safe, at least for the moment. A rattlesnake couldn't strike unless it was coiled, and could strike only the length of its coil. This one was already well behind him and slithering away rapidly, more afraid than Fargo was.

The problem, Fargo suddenly realized, was that the rattler was making a beeline toward the very spot where the Ovaro was still lying down. And Fargo dare not move suddenly to stop it, not while he was in the direct line of sight of the four men below.

He knew the stallion would not run off in a panic and desert his master. But even the best horse was still only a horse—instincts would take over if the Ovaro sensed the presence of a natural enemy.

Only a few heartbeats later, that's exactly what happened.

Nickering loudly in sudden fright, the stallion twisted up onto its feet, reared up, and began trying to crush the snake with his sharp front hoofs.

"Christ," Fargo muttered even as all four faces below snapped up toward his general direction.

He had no foolish ideas about trying to fight it out, especially without his Henry to hand. Instead, before the men could react, Fargo rolled himself up onto more solid ground and rose to his knees, Colt leaping into his fist.

He emptied every bean in the wheel, fanning the hammer to send a rapid spray of lead that forced the men to dive for cover.

Then he leaped up and sprinted hard toward his agitated horse, snatching up his hat as he flew past it. Fargo still had about ten paces to go, elbows and knees pumping frantically, when a withering volley of fire erupted behind him.

"Put at him, boys!" Ace Ludlow shouted the moment Fargo had emptied his gun and started running for his life.

Ace cursed his own luck—he had two coin-packed shotgun shells in his shirt pocket instead of in the breech of the gun. By the time he got it loaded, Fargo would be out of effective shotgun range.

He tossed the scattergun aside and slapped for his five-shot revolver. Zeke Barlow and Hoyt had already locked their repeating rifles into their shoulder sockets and were busting caps as fast as they could rack rounds into the chamber.

Only Jack Duran moved slowly, almost leisurely, smiling with grim satisfaction as he lowered the breechblock on his Sharps Big Fifty. He seemed more intent on watching Fargo flee than on loading his weapon.

"Jack!" Ace roared. "Jack, goddamnit! Drop him with your Sharps!"

Duran thumbed a long cartridge into the chamber, closed the breechblock, threw the big buffalo gun into his shoulder. His mouth twisted like a sullen cur's as he began taking up the trigger slack.

"Oh, he ain't going out *that* easy, boss. I'm carving that bastard for a long time. I'll drop his mount right now, it's a bigger target. Then we'll toss the net over Fargo."

The Ovaro had become bullet-savvy from his travels with his master. The moment rounds began kicking up dirt and snapping off tree limbs, the stallion had gentled itself, knowing from experience that a hard run was ahead.

Fargo, rounds literally chewing into his clothing, didn't bother with a stirrup. He ran straight at the Ovaro's rump, leaped, used both strong arms to vault into the saddle, and thumped the pinto's ribs with his boot heels even before he snatched up the reins.

Assuming he survived this initial volley, Fargo had two immediate priorities. He *must* get beyond the range of Ace's deadly scattergun, which wouldn't take long, and Jack Duran's famously accurate Big Fifty, which would.

In fact, Fargo realized, it would take far too long. There was little leeway, in this dense path, to ride an avoidance pattern. And Duran would know to aim for the horse—a big, easy target up to at least two hundred yards for a Big Fifty. And they were not even half that distance away yet.

Fargo had no time to debate. He reacted instantly, slipping his feet out of the stirrups, placing one hand on the saddle horn, and the other on the cantle. He lifted himself up, twisted halfway around, and dropped backward into the saddle. It was an awkward angle, but in less than three seconds he was still retreating at a gallop, yet facing his enemy.

He snatched his Henry from its saddle boot even as a round flumped into his blanket roll and another tore a chunk out of his left boot heel. More bullets caused a steady blow-fly drone as they screamed past his ears.

But Fargo ignored the repeated brush of death's wings and focused all his senses down to the main threat: Jack Duran, and that Big Fifty he was now notching on the Ovaro.

Once again Fargo and the stallion's fate depended on the

Henry's superior tooling and magazine capacity. The weapon was cumbersome to load, but B. Tyler Henry's automatic breech-feeding mechanism functioned like Swiss gears. No matter how rapidly Fargo worked the lever, the next shot was ready with no hint of a stoppage or hang fire.

And he worked it with demonic speed now, knowing that only a virtual wall of lead stood between him and eternity. He *had* to give his fleet stallion enough time to open a good lead.

The rifle stock repeatedly slapping his cheek, hot brass shell casings raining around him, Fargo peppered Jack Duran's position and hoped he wasn't too late.

Jack Duran was on the feather edge of dropping Fargo's stallion when, in a welter of confusion, he realized his "fleeing" enemy was facing him and drawing a bead on him!

Duran got the shot off, but was so startled he jerked the trigger and bucked his gun.

This astounding feat of circus riding was totally unexpected and rocked all four men back on their heels.

"*Ho*-ly shit! He's got wheels on his ass!" shouted Hoyt Jackson just before the first rounds chunked into the dirt walls surrounding them. "Hit the deck!"

At first, all four men hunkered down in a panic. But not one round even came that close—Fargo, they realized, had just successfully tossed a scare into them to cover his retreat.

Duran leaped to his feet, cussing a blue streak.

"The death hug's a-comin', Fargo!" he shouted behind the escaping man. "You can carve that in granite! I'll wear your guts for garters, you bastard!"

"Save it, Jack," Ace snapped, hatred and malice burning in his eyes as he slapped dirt off his trousers. "I've had my belly full of that sneaky son of a bitch. Now he's sniffed out our tunnel, it's time to end it before he puts the word out."

"Tonight?" Duran demanded.

Ace nodded. "We're going back after him. Me, you, Hoyt, and Zeke. And this time we *will* put the quietus on him."

9

"Augh!" Snowshoe Hendee roared out in greeting as Fargo rode into camp about a half hour before sunset. "You're *still* above the ground, Skye? Or should I call you Lazarus? They was enough racket, comin' from Lewis's River, to wake snakes. Bleeding Holy Ghost! Your buckskins is shot full o' holes. Wing ya?"

"Nah, but it got lively," Fargo admitted as he swung down and began stripping the tack from his pinto. "Think I found the entrance to their hideout. How'd it go up here? Any visitors?"

"Nobody I had to shoot. Only Ruck-a-Chucky. Prac'ly bawled like a baby when I said you was gone. He left a string of trout. Says he'll be back to see you. Also said they was two more prospectors murdered and robbed last night. One right here in the Seven Devils, the other just north of Summit Ridge."

Fargo's lips compressed in a frown. "Both in or near Hell's Canyon."

"A-huh. One had his head crushed by a rock, the other was throat-slashed—so deep the gullet was severed, Chucky says."

"That second one you mentioned," Fargo said tonelessly as he stripped off the saddle blanket and pad, "would most likely be the handiwork of Jack Duran, the back-shooting 'occasional barber.' Also 'pears he's sworn a personal vendetta against me."

"Agin' *you*?" Snowshoe chuckled as he bit off a chew and got it juicing. "This hoss never could understand suicide. Mayhap Duran'll change his thinking. Be smarter to butt-kick a sore-tailed grizz."

" 'Smart' ain't high on a man's list," Fargo retorted, "once he's got blood in his eyes."

This time out the Ovaro had indeed worked up a sweat, and his bit was flecked with foam. The wind was turning cold, so Fargo quickly rubbed the stallion down with an old feed sack to dry him before turning him out to graze with the four team horses.

"Yonder comes that cute little button Tammy," Snowshoe said. "She's been a-frettin' and a-steamin' ever since that shooting scrape earlier, worried 'bout you."

Tammy was out of breath from running up the slope, and her deep breathing further emphasized the bursting swell of her bodice. She wore a thin muslin dress that flattered her figure, and she didn't seem to mind the two men's eyes enjoying the sight.

"Skye! Thank God you're all right. I was worried sick."

She flashed him a toothy smile, smoothing her dress with both hands and pulling it tighter on top. The air was turning brisk, and Fargo saw where her wind-stiffened nipples dinted the fine fabric. It caused him a flush of loin heat when he recalled last night, and the maddening pleasure as she raked her eyeteeth along his hard shaft.

"Like my dress?" she asked him, preening. "I wore it special for you."

"Damn, boy," Snowshoe whispered, "you musta trimmed her good, uh?"

"You look pretty as four aces," Fargo assured her.

"Some fellas says my legs is real nice, for a short gal," Tammy added. "Think?"

With a mischievous little smile, she hiked the dress up scandalously high, exposing her bare, supple legs well past the middle of her creamy thighs.

She then blew a kiss at Fargo, turned, and hurried back toward her own camp.

"Supper's near ready," she called without looking back.

Both men kept their eyes in motion, trying not to be distracted by the pretty young thing walking away from them as they watched the terrain, making the vital calculations familiar to frontiersmen. And both were silently deciding how tonight's inevitable attack would come. The sun was hardly more than a ruddy afterthought on the western horizon, and dark shadows were spreading like ink stains across the surrounding lower slopes of the Seven Devils Mountains.

"Let's grab some grub now," Fargo suggested. "That fish smells good. Besides, they won't move on us until full dark."

"A-huh. Jump us in our bedrolls, likely."

Both men headed downslope.

"It's true that greedy Chucky ain't helping matters around here none," Snowshoe opined. "But you know, Skye? I been studying on it. It's this fiend-begotten custom of preemption what starts all the troubles. Makes these pilgrims get pushy. It's just stealing with a fancy name."

Fargo had to agree. Squatters back in the Plains assumed preemption privilege, the right to pay later for any land they occupied and claimed exclusive title to. Encroaching prospectors out here tossed the phrase around, too.

"It's not much different with this damn 'statehood' movement," Fargo said. "It's just a trumped-up smokescreen to hide the powerful land speculators. There's plenty others like us who think the Western territory should be a common national treasure. But since the land barons got Congress in their hip pocket, so-called 'statehood' is really just all about breaking the West up into profit bundles."

"Speak the truth and shame the devil," Snowshoe agreed. " 'Nuff to frost your nuts, ain't it?"

"Yeah, but don't forget. The pilgrims may be a pain in the ass, greedy and green. But Ace Ludlow and his bunch are the thieves and killers."

"A-huh, that shines. And we'd be fools to think they wish us a peaceful sleep tonight—'ceptin' maybe the permanent kind."

Earlier, Snowshoe had filleted the trout Ruck-a-Chucky brought and showed the women how to wrap it in peppered leaves to bake directly in hot ashes. The meat flaked off in tender morsels, the first good meal Fargo had enjoyed in days.

Throughout supper Tammy hovered jealously near Fargo, resentful of the attention the other girls paid him. However, it was Mattie Everett Fargo studied most closely. She seemed less openly hostile toward Fargo, but nervous and on edge. Every sound, from beyond the comforting glow of the campfire, made her start nervously.

Near the end of the meal, Fargo said, "Expecting somebody, Mattie?"

She stared at him, anger sparking in her eyes. Like him, she kept her voice low so the rest couldn't hear them.

"You ask a lot of questions as if you have a right to do so, Mr. Fargo."

"When your lover boy tries to pump me full of lead," Fargo told her, "that makes it my business."

The encroaching night made it difficult to read her face. Fargo had meant to get a telltale reaction from her. But she didn't rise to the bait.

"Is this a riddle?" she asked.

"No, but Ace Ludlow is the lowest form of murdering scum that ever hatched from a snake's egg. And I'll tell you flat out: As much as I admire the fair sex, I would show no mercy to *any* woman who helped that butcher hurt those four girls in any way."

Fargo had blindsided her, yet she hardly reacted. But remember, he told himself, if Mattie is Ace's female partner, that means she's a good flimflam artist.

"Fine by me," she replied. "I have no idea who Ace Ludlow is, nor any desire to hurt the girls."

She spoke that last sentence, Fargo noticed, with more conviction than she put in her denial of knowing Ace.

"Speaking of not hurting the girls . . . made up your mind yet, Mattie?"

"About what?"

"North to Fort Walla Walla or south to Fort Bridger."

"I *told* you, my mind's been made up on that score. All five of us gave our word of honor to our future husbands. We shall wait right here for them."

"This Mr. Chandler and the rest of your . . . fiancés—they must never leave their plush houses in nearby Chandlerville, huh?"

Mattie said nothing to this barb, merely casting her eyes demurely downward.

Fargo said mildly, "You keep plenty of secrets, Mattie. Maybe you have to—or *think* you have to. Just remember, you got to live with the decisions you make. And accept the consequences."

"I have no idea what you're talking about."

"I think you do," Fargo retorted. "But something or

somebody's got you scared. And since you're of no mind to make a choice, I'm making it for you. As soon as your horses have grazed up a little more, we push north to Fort Walla Walla."

"What?" Mattie demanded.

"We got possibly hostile redskins to the south plus the lava-bed country to skirt. So we'll go north."

"That's kidnapping!" she protested.

"Not if I'm saving those other four from rape and murder," he said bluntly, this time staring her down.

"Good night," she said stiffly, rising in a rustle of skirts and hurrying in a huff toward the celerity wagon. Fargo couldn't help thinking about that Colt Navy and the wisdom of letting her keep it.

"She got a pinecone up her butt again?" Tammy asked, moving closer to Fargo around the fire.

He started soaping his saddle in the flickering firelight. "She doesn't like me too much, I guess."

"Well, honey, I sure do. Can we maybe have more pie later tonight?" She smiled mischievously at him.

Reluctantly, Fargo shook his head. "If I was ever tempted. But not tonight. Matter fact, make sure you go nowhere near my bedroll. It may get warm, all right, but not like last night."

Tammy's pretty face formed a pout. "Maybe I'll change your mind."

Fargo was about to warn her again when a peal of sudden, silly giggles from the other side of the fire caught his attention.

Snowshoe was leaning back against a big rock, grinning like a sultan in his harem. The Papenhagen twins, Hilda and Helga, had finished their usual tandem ritual of brushing their teeth with willow twigs. Now each of them was combing out one of Snowshoe's twin beard braids. They retwisted them and tied them in pink ribbons. One girl was perched at each of his knees. Their hair shone like burnished gold in the firelight.

"Glad now I scrubbed you, stinkweed?" Fargo called over.

"Ah, go crap in your hat, Fargo!"

Despite now smelling sweeter to the ladies, Snowshoe was still irked at his friend. On the way to supper, Fargo

84

had tripped the old trapper into the runoff stream and soaped him up good. The women stood by laughing and cheering—even Mattie had cracked a rare smile.

"How did you get the name 'Snowshoe'?" the twin at his left knee asked. Fargo didn't know which one she was—he couldn't tell them apart when they were dressed.

"On account I'm a true Nor'wester, that's how. During winters, this hoss stays up here even when it snows so deep the rabbits suffocate in their burrows. But I just tie big paddles on my boots and go 'bout my business. So folks call me Snowshoe."

"You have a nice face," she pronounced. "Careworn, but full of character."

"Still got my teeth, too. Leastways, the ones what ain't been knocked out at ronnyvoos on the Green River."

"What's your real name?" asked the other twin, adjusting the bow just right in his pink ribbon.

Snowshoe winked at her. "Gi'me a little sugar, mayhap I'll tell you."

Both twins giggled as one. Damn, thought Fargo. I'll bet those gals do *everything* together. He grinned, wondering if Snowshoe realized that. But what a way to go. . . .

"Don't you even like to know a girl before you . . . get cozy with her, gramps?" Tammy called over.

"I hope to get to know all five of you," Snowshoe assured her. "In the Old Testament sense."

The twins both twittered.

"Snowshoe," teased the twin at his left knee, "you're *shame*less! A gent your age, talking that way. Just how old are you, anyway?"

"Le' me see. . . ."

Snowshoe tugged at one of his beard braids. "Don't go by this craggy face. I'uz a young buck when I come up here."

"When was that?"

"Six months ago," he replied, showing no trace of a smile.

"Ladies," Fargo chimed in, "that old relic's been around since God was in short britches."

"Fargo, you *had* teeth when you got here," Snowshoe warned him. "These two little fillies is *my* cavvy. Go wrangle your own."

Instead, Fargo took a little walk out onto the slopes to bring the horses in closer to camp. He was sure an attack of some kind was coming later, and killing the horses would be high on the gang's list.

When he returned to the camp circle, Yvette, the coffee-and-cream-complected Creole beauty, was practicing a theatrical scene for the rest. The moment Fargo arrived, she drew close to him and began performing a sort of sensual, sinewy dance of the seven veils. Her eyes held his as she moved her hips in a slow, provocative, thrusting motion that made his breathing quicken.

"You shameless Jezebel!" Tammy exploded. "I heard how the women in New Orleans are all fast."

"This is art, you bumpkin!" Yvette flung back.

She had begun writing a play yesterday. Now she gazed longingly into Fargo's eyes and broke into a melodramatic monologue from it.

"No, ladies, no! Never, *never* must we succumb to the black dog of despair! While yet there rides one pure and brave man on a noble steed, hope burns bright in my bosom!"

Still gazing at Fargo, she cast a tragic sigh, swelling that burning bosom even more.

This was too rich for Snowshoe. He sputtered with laughter, spraying tobacco juice all over the twins. Tammy, too, began howling with mirth.

"Skye Fargo, *pure*?" Snowshoe howled at the moon. "Frenchie, you are a caution to screech owls. He's 'bout as 'pure' as yellow snow."

"Whack the cork, you old reprobate," Fargo said.

Yvette, miffed at everyone, was suddenly on her dignity. She stared at Tammy like a cat ready to pounce.

"*Mon Dieu!* I should know better than to cast pearls to swine. What would a hillbilly harlot know about interpretive dance or acting?"

Tammy started to fly up, but Fargo grabbed her.

"Speaking of acting," he teased Yvette, "what did you think of that 'untutored bachelor of the forest,' Ruck-a-Chucky? Did you catch his voices and accents? I could put him on tour back East, get rich."

"Jesus," muttered Snowshoe, "don't tell *him* that."

But Fargo, glancing up at the rising moon, knew the time

for small talk was over. He and Snowshoe had a few items to discuss before Ace Ludlow's bunch sent in their cards.

"Gettin' late, ladies," he announced. "Best turn in now. And stay close to camp."

He stood up, hefting his newly soaped saddle and his Henry.

"I mean that," he said, holding Tammy's gaze. "*Stick close to camp.* Might get dangerous up near our spot."

Fargo and Snowshoe were no strangers to shooting scrapes. As they strolled back toward their camp, both men silently studied the moonlit landscape. No doubt stone-hearted killers would soon be slinking across it like sneaking coyotes. But the old friends eased into the topic gradually.

"Skeeters ain't hatched yet, nor flies," Snowshoe remarked. "Good time for man *and* hoss. Hell, look—your stallion ain't had to switch his tail once."

Snowshoe spat a streamer of tobacco juice. "Grass could be better, though," he admitted. "Patchy. Still too close to winter; ain't filled in yet. But leastways there ain't no johnsongrass hereabouts to loco our mounts. Hell, that mule of mine has made do with sagebrush. Now *there's* some tough fodder, chum."

"This ain't the worse place to hole up," Fargo agreed. "High ground, open approaches, plenty of water, a few days' graze left. But it just might become necessary to move those gals, maybe at night in a hurry. If that happens, can we use your camp on the river as a fallback?"

Snowshoe nodded. "What, you thinkin' they might just skip us, go right for the women?"

Fargo shook his head. "Not right off. Not until they kill me first. Don't forget, now I know where the entrance to their hideout is. They can't relax until I'm dead."

"Then how's come you think we might hafta move the gals?"

"You're growing soft between the head handles, old timer. Everything I just said assumes the gang stays disciplined, under their leader Ace Ludlow's orders. But what happens to a snake when its head gets crushed?"

"It goes to thrashing ever which way," Snowshoe replied, nodding. "I take your drift. There's prime woman flesh just a-sittin' here like ripe fruit on the vine. Happens Ace's boys do fix his flint, them horny sons-a-bitches'll go hog wild."

"They'll be all over this place," Fargo said. "Loaded for bear and guns blazing, to hell with discretion. Your camp would just be a fallback. I might have to clear those gals outta this entire region fast."

"A-huh. Them women's the whole shootin' match. But as to gettin' out fast . . . that-'ere conveyance they got ain't worth its weight. Reason there ain't even a short-line stage around here yet is there ain't no damn roads for one."

"That's why I mentioned your camp," Fargo said. "It's not roads I have in mind. Are you *sure* you sealed that skiff tight?"

Snowshoe chuckled, then spat amber. He shook his head in admiration.

"Fargo, you son of trouble, I shoulda knowed you was planning a fandango. Likely, you'll get me kilt. But it *will* be a show, by the Lord Harry! Yessir, Skye, that-'ere skiff is sealed awfully tight. 'Course, Lewis's River bein' the way it is, it might do the gang's work for 'em. Pick your poison."

"That cannon might get useful, too," Fargo mused. "Especially since it's portable."

By now they had reached their separate camp, high up the slope but somewhat wind-sheltered in a swale between hummocks.

"But we've got tonight to worry about right now," Fargo added.

"A-huh. Mainly it's Ace and that goldang scattergun o' his'n. These bedroll killers is almost as green as pilgrims; we'll know before they're on us. But a man don't need much skill when a double-ten's loaded like Ace loads it."

"Yeah. So we'll switch off on guard duty," Fargo said. "I'll take the first watch. We'll run a length of twine between each other and tie it around our wrists so who ever's on guard can shake the other awake without making any noise."

Despite Snowshoe's well-advanced age and strange quirks, Fargo trusted him completely. The old salt was a trail-savvy survivor trained by the first generation of mountain men. Like Fargo, he took his clues from the wind and the birds and the insects, from the little sounds that didn't belong to a place, the silences that were too deep for too long.

"Oh, there'll be a ronnyvoo, all right," Snowshoe said as he laid his Hawken gun out on the ground beside his buffalo robes. "Might even come down to cold steel 'fore the dance is over."

Snowshoe pulled a short, broad-bladed Spanish dag from his sash. "Won it from a don down in Old Mex. Lookit how there's blood gutters carved deep into the blade. Bleeds a man out quicker."

Snowshoe crawled into his robes, then farted. "Kiss for ya, Fargo."

"Rot in hell, Methuselah."

Fargo pulled a length of twine from one of his saddlebags.

Fargo wrapped the twine around his left hand so it would play out behind him as he walked. Then he picked up his Henry and moved out into the moonlit darkness, waiting for whomever was coming to test his mettle.

10

The temperature fell, the wind picked up, and the blood-orange moon slowly climbed toward its zenith.

The four killers—Ace Ludlow, Jack Duran, Hoyt Jackson, and Zeke Barlow—had tethered their horses back near the river. Now the men were sheltered in a little stand of scrub pine just below the women's camp.

"Fargo's been spelled by the old geezer," Zeke Barlow reported. "Won't be a better time than now, boss. Fargo's in his bedroll."

Ace nodded, teeth chattering despite his warm greatcoat. Zeke had been sent up the slope several times to make scouting reports. They had been forced to stand around in the cold waiting for Fargo to turn in. Nobody wanted to brace him while he was awake.

"All right, boys," Ace said, sliding his Paterson Colt from its hand-tooled holster and spinning the cylinder with his palm to check the action. "We don't want this done slap-dash. You seen it earlier today—this Fargo is savage as a meat ax. Give that son of a bitch one inch of slack, he'll hang you with it. Zeke?"

"Yo!"

"The old man is yours. Take him down quiet with that skull-cracker. And make sure he don't see another sunrise."

Ace meant the stone war club Zeke had claimed as a trophy after shooting a Sioux during a raid on the former muleteer's pack train out near Bozeman.

"Don't worry, boss. This little puppy could knock an elephant into the middle of next week."

Zeke held the club out so the rest could admire it in the

moonlight. A smooth stone the size of a man's fist had been wedged into the fork of an eighteen-inch haft. It was lashed tight with rawhide thongs that had been tied on soaking wet, then left to dry and shrink in the sun.

"A blacksmith couldn't knock that stone loose," Ace reminded them. "Hoyt, Jack—you're both going to team up on that lanky bastard."

Ace nodded toward the hardwood ax handle Hoyt carried. "Remember—we want no gunplay 'less it can't be avoided. Hoyt, you're a strong son of a buck. Just bean him a good one with that ax handle. If that don't quite kill him, the rest is Jack's play. Just so it gets done."

Jack Duran stroked his sheathed razor. "That plan suits me right down to the ground."

"Just remember," Ace cautioned. "The reason I'm sending a team in is just in case Fargo wakes up before Hoyt can conk him on the noggin. Noise or no noise, Jack, if that happens, use this."

Ace handed Duran his double-ten express gun with the specially loaded shells.

"Oh, *hell* yeah," Duran approved, accepting the weapon. "I'd prefer to peel him slow with my razor. Layer by layer, like an onion. But blasting him into stew meat with this will do just fine."

"Anything goes wrong," Ace added, "it's every man for himself. Hightail it back to the horses. Speaking of horses . . . any way we could hamstring that stallion of his, Zeke? Good insurance in case we don't kill Fargo tonight."

"Can't risk it," Zeke replied. "Fargo's brought it in too close. If it whickers, he might wake up."

"Hold on a minute," Hoyt put in. "While we're all doing our jobs, Ace, where you plan to be. Sittin' on your duff?"

"No, you dumb galoot. I told you earlier—I have to see can I talk to Mattie."

"Why?" Hoyt demanded. "Christ sakes, we're about to turn Fargo's brains into paste. We don't need Mattie for that."

Ace forced himself to keep his temper in check. "Hoyt, you're enough to vex a saint. Use your think piece, wouldja? We've *got* to get word to Mattie in case the cards don't fall our way tonight. If we don't get Fargo on that slope, Mattie will have to do it for us."

"Mattie! If *we* can't do for the bastard, how can she?"

"He's a man, ain't he? Mattie's got looks, quality blood, and breeding. He won't look for her to walk up behind him and blow his brains all over his breakfast."

"Ace is right," Duran said. "This jasper Fargo obviously plans to live a long life. He ain't gonna make this a bird's nest on the ground for us."

"*Now* you're whistling," Ace approved. "Damnit, boys, the son of a bitch has located our hideout! We can't leave this to chance now."

This time Fargo was having *the* erotic dream of his life.

It began in a delicious waft of honeysuckle perfume, as he lay face down in his bedroll. Deft, knowledgeable hands worked his buckskin trousers. Then he felt his dream lover straddle his rear like it was a saddle. She pushed his shirt up high and leaned down to tickle his bare back with hard, pointy nipples.

"Mmm," Fargo moaned in his sleep, forced to raise his hips to accommodate a furious erection.

Long hair tickled his neck and cheeks as his fantasy visitor licked and nibbled his ears. His erection forced Fargo to roll sideways, tugging the blanket off him. A sudden lick of cold wind on bare flesh shocked him awake.

But the "dream woman" was still there, warm and soft, as real as the boner she'd given him.

"Damnit, Tammy," he said, nudging her off so he could roll over and confront her. "I thought I told—"

Surprised, Fargo fell silent when he glimpsed the naked Creole beauty in the moonlight.

"*Bonsoir*, Skye," Yvette greeted him. "Disappointed it's not Tammy?"

He took in her luscious, beautifully sculpted breasts capped by huge, cocoa-colored nipples. She was slender and flat-bellied, with a copious thatch of hair between her legs. Those big, wing-shaped eyes watched him as she reached down and opened herself so he could see her swollen pearl.

"Disappointed?" he repeated. "Not hardly. Darlin', when the corral is filled with prime mares, a studhorse never plays favorites. But that ain't the point."

Fargo had to force his eyes off her so he could remember the damn point.

"Honey, you little fool. There could be killers notching their sights on us right now. Is that damned old goat asleep out there? How'd you get past him?"

Fargo glanced down. The twine was still tied to his wrist.

"Snowshoe?" Yvette laughed and snuggled in closer to Skye, one hand gripping his shaft. "He only asked if I would visit him, when you and I are finished, and 'wind his clock.' He is an earthy man, *non*? Strong and masterful like you."

"He's a damned old mule-headed fool is what he is. He shoulda sent you right back to your camp."

But her hand was working magic on him, and Skye felt himself weakening in that old, familiar way.

"I am surprised it's you and not Tammy," he admitted. "I half-expected her to disobey me."

"That ignorant hillbilly? I put a few drops of Miss Pinkham's Lotion in her coffee at supper. She'll sleep like a kitten all night. But *we* won't, Skye, will we?"

"Jesus, that's nice," he told her, hot tickles of pleasure shooting through his shaft as she expertly encircled it with just thumb and forefinger, squeezing tight. This concentrated all the pleasure in one tight little ring that moved from base to tip, base to tip, more and more rapidly.

Her breath was hot and damp as she cooed in his ear, her voice husky with wanting him: "Tammy brags about how she can please a man. But she is not a student of the art of love as I am."

Fargo felt a throbbing, insistent heat gathering steam below as her hand picked up speed and power like a pleasure piston.

"The—the art of love?" he repeated, ending on a little groan of encouragement.

"*Mais oui*. Acting is only a hobby, not my true passion. Have you heard of the Kamasutra?"

"No. But I got an inquiring nature, especially if you're the teacher."

"From the Kamasutra," she promised him in a throaty whisper, "I have learned to do things I'm sure no woman has ever done to you."

Secretly, Fargo considered that a mighty tall order. He'd had his back clawed by minister's daughters and gambler's whores, school teachers, nurses, newspaper reporters and even a Cheyenne princess. He'd had women young and old, short and tall, sassy and shy. Had them every way, in every position.

But, damnit, he liked a gal with ambition. Let her step up to the firing line and take her best shot.

"The Kamasutra, huh?" he said. "Well, I should be escorting you back to your camp; this ain't the time and place for fooforaw. But you've got me . . . ahh, curious. Hold off just a minute."

If he was going to be a damned fool, Fargo at least intended a good look around first. He could see Snowshoe's shadowy form about twenty yards out—the old lecher had sneaked in closer to eavesdrop on the coupling.

Fargo looked closely at the surrounding moonwashed slopes. But he also listened. The broad-leave trees below the pine belt were not yet in foliage, so there was a strange, empty stillness when the wind blew except for the distant, mournful whistle up in the caprock well above them.

It didn't feel right, somehow. Fargo's "goose tickle" was back—that cool prickling of his scalp when danger lurked nearby.

"Skye?" Yvette's silken whisper tempted him. "I know how to do things. Special things with the way I squeeze a man when he is inside me. Here, let me get on top and show you."

Not a wise idea, an inner voice warned Fargo. *The worst hurt in the world is out there on those slopes.*

But Yvette's exciting promise drowned out that voice: *I know how to do things. Special things . . .*

"Hell, Snowshoe's out there," Fargo muttered.

He made sure his Colt and Henry were within arm's length. Then he stretched out on his back and watched Yvette straddle him in the buttery moonlight.

"Get ready," she promised. "This will be a voyage for us both."

Fargo stifled a grin. Cute little thing, always being so melodramatic. Probably, she'd had two or three men and thought she was a regular courtesan. He told himself to make sure he praised her afterward, so she'd think . . . she'd think . . . *Jesus!*

Fargo's train of thought was derailed when she expertly bent him to the perfect entry angle, raised herself up to clear his length, then nudged just his purple-swollen tip into the heat of her belly mouth.

Delicious heat and tight, velvety pressure sent shudders of pleasure through him. Gasping at the explosive contact, Yvette took more of him inside her. And now Fargo realized she hadn't just been boasting about special things she could do to a man.

Her talented inner muscle milked his member. Squeeze, release, squeeze, release, sque-e-eze . . . Fargo began to roll his head and moan, unable to contain the gathering pleasure. It felt like every nerve ending in his shaft was being kissed by warm, silken lips.

Squeeze, release, squeeze, release, sque-e-eze . . .

"That's not all," she promised, reaching one hand down to cup him between his legs.

Fargo had been fondled and touched before. But now a true erotic virtuoso had him in hand. Even as her unbelievably flexible love muscle kneaded and squeezed his curved saber, her magic fingers fired a hot, thrumming pleasure down below.

"Oh, *there*, I feel it cooking down there, Skye," she gasped, so excited herself that she was pounding up and down on him like a bronc rider. "Oh, I feel you getting hard as steel inside me, too! Oh, oh, *mon Dieu!* All for you, for you, take me higher, Skye, *high*er! Oh, I'm—I'm— ahh, *ahh, ahhiiieee* . . . !"

Losing all control, shrieking without awareness of others hearing, Yvette climaxed.

"NOW!" she screamed, giving Fargo a final squeeze that blew open his floodgates. With several powerful, conclusive thrusts, he spent himself deep inside her.

Neither one of them had the energy to even move for several minutes. Both lay gasping as if they'd been running for hours. When awareness finally replaced his spent daze, Fargo rose up on one elbow.

Snowshoe was still out there, although it looked like the nosy old fart was shaking with silent laughter.

" 'I feel it *cooking* down there?' " Snowshoe quoted amidst sputtering laughter, just loud enough for Fargo to hear. "Boy, you've bulled some lulus in your day."

"Go stroke your Whore of Babylon, you old Satyr."

Well, nosy or no, it was good to have Snowshoe out there, Fargo thought. Because Yvette's hand was working its deft magic on him again. And the savvy little vixen already had him past the point of stopping her.

Mattie Everett was returning to the celerity wagon after making a quick necessary trip. She stepped clear of a little copse of pines just as a shadowy form blocked her path.

"Ace!" she exclaimed. "You frightened me!"

"That's good. Shows you got a brain in that pretty head."

He swept her into his arms and brutally kissed her mouth, his hands pinching and squeezing everything she had.

" 'S'matter?" he demanded. "I felt you pulling back from me just now, woman. Ain't you glad to see your lovin' man?"

His tone was brutal, mocking, husky with pent-up lust. Mattie had learned long ago that Ace Ludlow was the devil incarnate. But she had made the stupid, youthful mistake of getting mixed up with him because he seemed "exciting," so different from her prim and proper upbringing. Now his hold over her was absolute.

"Of course I'm glad to see you, Ace," she replied, forcing the loathing from her tone. "It's just . . . you startled me."

"How's this for 'startling' you, sugar?"

Ace slapped her hard. So hard it staggered her sideways and left her ears ringing.

"You goddamn, high-toned *bitch*," he hissed. "The hell you think you're doing, huh? *Look* at me, woman! This is two days now you been sittin' on your fancy pratt while that bastard Fargo killed two of my men. You still got that gun I gave you?"

"Y-yes, but—"

" 'But' don't feed the bulldog, you sniveling little bitch. Hell, you ain't some helpless virgin. You coulda killed him by now easier than rolling off a log."

Ace grabbed Mattie's shoulders so hard she cried out in pain.

"Is it cuz that bastard's poking you, Mattie?"

"No, Ace! I swear!"

Ace slapped her again. "You're *mine*, do you mark me, woman? You carry my brand all over that sweet body, inside and out. And *no* man drives Ace Ludlow's stock, hear me?"

"Ace, I swear, I never—"

"And you better not, cuz you know I'll kill you. But first I'll write some letters, destroy that highfalutin family of yours back in Virginia. That Bible-thumping, teetotal father of yours—a preacher man gettin' into politics, huh? Wait'll word gets out his sweet little girl is a notorious express-coach robber. And an outlaw's whore, to boot. His pedestal won't be so high then, think?"

"No, Ace, please! I swear I've done nothing to help this man Fargo and never would. He just imposed himself on us."

That much Ace believed. Fargo seemed to "impose himself" on just about everybody.

"Then, damnit," he said, "kill him."

"Kill him?"

"Did I stutter, you stupid cow? Yes, assuming my men don't get him tonight, *you* kill him. Just put the gun in your clothes. Wait until you're behind him, then shoot him in the back of the head. Hell, it's easier 'n cooking a flapjack."

"For you. Ace, I—I've helped you steal money." Mattie faltered. "But never have I killed anyone."

"Hell, nobody has, girl, until their first time. You *will* shoot him, Mattie, hear me? The bastard's tossing a scare into my men. Besides, he knows where the hideout is, and I can't let him noise that around. And we *got* to get them women to the cabin before my men revolt on me. I got big plans, Mattie. I can ramrod this entire region if I play my hand smart. But you buck me, girl—"

Ace slipped both hands around her soft, slender white throat. He didn't squeeze hard—just enough to feel her pulse throbbing in his palms like the heart of a trapped bird. Just a little warning.

"Don't cross me, Mattie. If he's alive in the morning, you *kill* that son of a bitch."

While their boss laid in wait for Mattie, Hoyt and Jack had slowly made their way up the slope toward Fargo's separate little campsite.

Despite his white-hot, burning hatred and personal

grudge against Fargo, Duran wasn't feeling too brash right now. He had watched Fargo cheat death twice. This was a hard man to kill.

But as they inched closer through the grass, sounds began to reach Duran's ears. Sounds that could mean only one thing: big, bad Skye Fargo had just been caught with his pants down. The mighty Trailsman, as Zeke called him, playing slap and tickle with one of the gals and letting some fleabag old man protect him.

A man in the heat of the rut hardly had his senses focused on danger. Jack grinned. For once, he thought, maybe I was wrong. This *will* be a bird's nest on the ground.

They inched closer. Feminine moans reached their ears.

Jack elbowed Hoyt, and the two men exchanged a knowing grin. About twenty yards to their left, Duran could make out Zeke's form as he moved in on the feeble old fart with the Plains rifle.

"Let's go pay our respects," Duran whispered, and both men began inching forward again.

Yvette, Fargo realized in dazed wonder, had told no lies when she promised him a "voyage." They had already been around the world once, and were going for trip number two when Snowshoe suddenly tugged the twine tied around Fargo's wrist.

Tugged it hard and repeatedly.

Almost simultaneously, Snowshoe's big-caliber Hawken gun split the silence of the night like a thunderclap.

"Shit-fire! Ain't it the berries? Got me a spiffy new skull-cracker!" his gravely voice roared out in triumph. "And here's one more coal-shoveler for Satan, his guts hangin' out his bunghole! *Augh!*"

Fargo, however, was literally in no position to celebrate. The moment he felt the twine jerk, he flexed his muscles and rolled hard to the right, taking Yvette (whom he was still deep inside) with him.

Fargo actually felt the wind from it when Hoyt Jackson's ax handle smashed hard into the bedroll, right where Fargo's head had been a heartbeat earlier. But now he saw he had an even bigger problem, and he felt a ball of ice replace his stomach.

The very gun Fargo had vowed he never wanted to stare at was now staring at *him*. Both barrels, like cold, unblinking eyes. Jack Duran held the hell-spawned weapon, his mean little pinched face twisted with murderous hatred.

"Take one last look," Duran snarled. "A better man just killed you."

Duran's mistake, however, was in taking that extra few moments to gloat and rub Fargo's nose in it. That gave the Trailsman just enough time to snatch his Colt and cock it on its way out of the holster.

But Duran already had his gun leveled and his finger on the twin triggers. Fargo had no time whatsoever for anything but a hurried snapshot. The Colt bucked in his fist. He heard Duran suck in a fast breath, then scream hideously as Fargo's hasty shot grazed his jaw and tore off about half of his left ear.

The double-ten express gun did go off with a concussive roar that made Snowshoe's Hawken sound like a popgun. The blast momentarily deafened Fargo. But his bullet had knocked Duran back, causing the muzzle to lift with him. The lethal load of coins moth-holed one edge of Fargo's blanket and plowed a trench in the dirt beneath it.

Fargo was shaken but unhurt. However, Yvette's piercing screams made him fear she'd been tagged.

Luckily, they were in no immediate danger from Duran's partner. Duran's wound not only hurt like hell, forcing him to shrill screams almost like Yvette's, but Fargo's bullet had addled his brain when it grazed his jaw like a hard punch. He staggered like a man who had been slugged hard but not quite knocked out.

Hoyt Jackson was strong and dangerous, but not when he had to be the take-charge man. Duran's unexpected screaming panicked and confused Hoyt. He took the scattergun in one hand, Duran in the other, and led them on a dead run down the moonlit slope.

Fargo did not pursue them—not with a naked, hysterical, possibly wounded girl screaming blue murder beneath him and yet more panicky women shouting questions from the camp below.

It turned out Yvette was only frightened badly by the blast—thanks to Fargo's quick reflexes, she, too, had missed death by mere inches. They were both still pulling on their clothing when Snowshoe materialized beside them. His Hawken was still smoking as he ogled the half-naked Yvette. The stone war club filled his other hand.

"Sainted backsides!" he exclaimed, staring at the shredded blanket and the torn-up earth that marked the brunt of the blast. "Whew! Jumped over a snake that time, boy."

Fargo nodded. But what about next time, and the time after? That handheld house-leveler was looming large in his future, he realized.

"We can't let up on 'em," he said. "The one you just killed makes three, with another wounded. And the wounded man is Jack Duran, who's brain-sick and kill-crazy, not to mention nursing a grudge against me that's even bigger now. Face it, Ace is gonna have a coup on his hands unless he kills me—kills *us*, old-timer—mighty damn quick. So let's steal a march on him."

"Now you know where they are," Snowshoe suggested, "why bust a sweat? Why'n'cha just get word to the vigilantes?"

Fargo shook his head, still comforting Yvette, who was trembling like a rain-soaked kitten. She had gone into shock and paid no attention to the men.

"Some of these 'regulator' gangs," he told Snowshoe, "are better than no law at all. But others are just criminal trash using 'law and order' as eyewash to kill and rape and plunder. I've seen that bunch out in San Francisco. Damn bullyboys, that's all. We bring that kind into the mix, what chance you think these women stand?"

Snowshoe nodded, tugging at one of his beard braids.

"A-huh, that rings right. Them little blond twins ain't just good eats—they's both sweet gals. Be a shame, happens them filthy bastards of Ludlow's gets a-hold of any of them 'ere gals."

"That's why we ain't going to let up," Fargo said. "Sometimes it's smart to quarter the wind. Other times, it's best to head right into it. We fly the black flag now, old son. No surrender, no terms. Clear out or die."

Snowshoe grinned and waved the skull-cracker about. "*Hell*, yes! Might get me a Paiute warbonnet next time. Tomorrow?"

Fargo nodded. "Ace's rats like to hole up by day, strike at night. So let's pay them a little visit in the morning."

11

Things were tense around the women's campfire the next morning. In fact, even if Ace Ludlow's bunch never touched him, Skye Fargo wasn't sure he'd live to finish breakfast.

And mostly, he had to admit, it was his own damn stupid fault.

The night before, with Yvette's steamy talk egging him on, it had been easy to forget about hot-tempered Tammy. After all, she'd supposedly been dosed with laudanum. But the world-shaking blast from Ace Ludlow's double-ten had shocked even her awake. And naturally, all the women saw it when Fargo escorted a badly shaken Yvette back to camp, obviously naked under her linen shift.

Now both women's eyes were shooting daggers at each other, and Tammy's eyes at him. Fargo feared he was dog meat if he didn't walk on eggshells here. He wore no woman's brand, but he knew the rules: A man was a fool if he dallied with two women who know, and can't stand, each other.

None of this was wasted on devious Snowshoe, who wanted nothing more than to see his dear trail companion ripped to shreds in a humdinger of a catfight.

"Awful dang sorry, ladies," he said with oily politeness as he sipped coffee from a tin cup, " 'bout all that *noise* last night. Before the shootin' started, I mean. Skye here didn't mean to disturb you. You know what they say—the best stallions're the ones what neighs the loudest in the heat of desire."

Yvette cast her eyes demurely, yet proudly, downward as Tammy flushed with jealous anger. She turned almost the shade of her cinnamon braid and seemed on the verge of pouncing on Yvette, Fargo, or both.

"Keep it up, you old jackass," Fargo warned in a mutter, "and I swear I'll cut your tongue out. You're juggling dynamite."

Fargo glanced around. "Where's Mattie?"

"Why?" Tammy spat at him. "Your whore from New Orleans didn't work it enough for you last night?"

"*Ciel!* You ignorant, hayseed tramp!" Yvette shrieked, and in an eyeblink both women pounced at each other, clawing, kicking, slapping, pulling hair.

Snowshoe howled with gusto as Fargo, cursing, joined the twins in prying the combatants apart. Snowshoe had to roll onto his side, laughing so hard he gasped for breath, when a flying knee caught Fargo in the testicles, turning his face a sickly green above his beard.

"You like it, boy, so you pay for it!" he managed to taunt between howls of mirth.

"*Stop* this! Stop it at once, do you hear me?"

Mattie's voice was shrill, almost hysterical. She had just emerged from the conveyance, where mirrors were mounted on the inside door panels, and was still brushing out her hair.

The fight broke up and Snowshoe's laughing fit abruptly ended. Fargo noticed how, all of a sudden, everybody was acting like teacher had caught all of them passing notes in class. Mattie had that kind of effect on others. Why, he wondered, would a woman with her good looks and bearing do the bidding of Ace Ludlow? He had no proof she was, but all the clues were there.

"See what you've caused, Mr. Fargo?" she accused, whirling toward him with eyes ablaze. "No killers came prowling around us until *you* showed up to 'help.' And now you're driving a wedge between the girls! How long do you plan to keep running our lives for us?"

"As stubborn as I am," he replied, "I'd say until hell freezes over, and then maybe even a little while on the ice."

She withered under his close scrutiny, averting her eyes. The pretty face was lined with worry, and her desperation and fear were palpable. The woman was under extraordinary pressure, and that made her dangerous.

The morning air was crisp, and she wore a blue wool

shawl wrapped around her arms and shoulders. Both hands were tucked inside it.

For warmth, Fargo hoped, wondering again if he'd been stupid to let her keep that Colt Navy.

"It's true we had visitors up at our camp," he told her, his lake-blue gaze holding her brown eyes until once again she was forced to look away. "How 'bout you ladies?"

"Don't be ridiculous, Mr. Fargo. I notice you're very good at shifting the attention away from your own misdeeds."

She raised her chin indignantly, then turned her back on him and headed toward the runoff rill to perform her morning toilette. Fargo watched her, his eyes narrowing in speculation.

"Picturing her naked?" Tammy demanded. "Maybe *she'll* comfort you tonight. Cost you more'n a nickel, though, like last night's camp follower."

Oh, shit, Fargo thought when Yvette started to arch her back again. But one of the twins quickly spoke up.

"Skye? The rest of us, except for Mattie, agree with you now. There's no 'town' around here. We've been tricked somehow. We take our orders from you, not Mattie."

Despite their feud, even Tammy and Yvette nodded assent to this.

"That's Helga talkin'," Snowshoe muttered. "The one that's got the birthmark. She's also got that little freckle bridge on her nose that Hilda ain't."

"She told you about her birthmark?"

Snowshoe grinned, revealing teeth stained dark brown from tobacco. "Like hell, turd. She *showed* me. This child means to trim both them 'ere twins. Hell, me 'n' you is pards, and *you're* diddling two o' the gals, aintcher?" He winked and added, "I got them fillies lippin' salt outta my hand. Won't be long, they'll let me mount."

Snowshoe tilted his silver head in the direction Mattie had taken. "I'll flip ya fir the fiery-haired wench."

"When can we leave?" Helga added in a musical, plaintive voice. "We don't like it here. Hilda and I want to go home."

"I figure one more day's graze," Fargo told her, "and your team will be ready to push north. But I don't want to abandon this position while the gang is still a threat."

During all this discussion Mattie had returned. Fargo noticed how she studiously avoided his eyes while she poured herself coffee from the chipped-enamel pot and helped herself to a biscuit. Were her hands trembling from nerves or the chill?

"So what's on your mind besides your hat, Skye?" Snowshoe demanded. "You got a plan for this morning's attack, hey?"

Fargo glanced upslope, where the body of the man Snowshoe plugged last night would soon be marked by wheeling vultures. Except that it wouldn't be there long . . .

"A plan?" Fargo repeated. "I ain't one to change horses on the gallop, you know that. My plan from the start has been to nerve-rattle Ace's men. Criminals are lazy and cowardly by nature, that's why they choose their line. They won't stick for a hard fight, so we can't let up."

While the two men spoke in low voices, Fargo watched Mattie stand up. One hand still tucked behind her shawl, she picked up the coffeepot with the other. She started going around the circle, topping off cups.

Funny, Fargo thought. She'd never showed such personal servitude before—she let the younger gals do such things.

Mattie topped off Snowshoe's cup. She passed behind Fargo to get to the cup in his right hand. He held it out for her, but Mattie had hesitated for some reason.

Fargo kept his eyes on Mattie's shadow. Keeping his voice level, without turning around to look at her, he said, "Mattie?"

After a long pause: "What?"

"You cleaned that weapon of yours since you . . . bought it?"

"I—I've hardly fired it. Why would I need to clean it?"

"Doesn't matter if you've fired it. Matter fact, gun oil tends to turn gummy if a weapon's not fired. Best to clean and oil it fresh every so often."

"I'll remember that, Mr. Fargo."

Her voice sounded calm enough. But when Mattie tried to fill his cup, she began trembling so hard she dropped the pot. The contents splashed, sizzling and steaming, into the fire.

"Oh! Excuse me!"

Mattie hurried toward the celerity wagon.

"The hell's biting at her?" Snowshoe wondered.

"Guilty conscience, I hope," Fargo said, wondering how close he'd just played that bluff. "But nobody can help her if she won't let 'em."

"Look!" Yvette called out, pointing down toward the twisting meanders of the Snake. "Here comes that funny Indian, Ruck-a-Chucky."

The huge Modoc wore his sheepskin coat, and he rolled in the saddle as if his ass were perfectly round. He was singing something, but Fargo couldn't make out the lyrics. He admired the Appaloosa's smooth gait, almost as steady as a pacer.

"His hoss ain't just pretty," Snowshoe remarked. "That-'ere 'loosa can turn on a two-bit piece and give you fifteen cents in change."

By now Ruck-a-Chucky was far enough up the slope that Fargo could make out his song, beautifully rendered in a flawless Texas drawl:

> *"Oh, pray for the ranger, you kindhearted stranger.*
> *He has roamed the prairies for many a year.*
> *He has kept the Comanches from off your ranches,*
> *And guarded your homes o'er the far frontier."*

Snowshoe chuckled and spat an amber streamer. "Hell, that red son of the Sierra ain't never seed a Comanch *nor* a ranger, much less Texas. I'd wager he heerd that song one time and now he's got 'er by heart. I swear, a parrot is poor fixin's 'longside Chucky."

Ruck-a-Chucky, a grin wreathing his homely moon face, raised one arm in greeting as his horse trotted into camp. He was munching roasted acorns from a fiber sack tied to his saddle horn. The Modoc always showed too many teeth when he smiled, a trait Fargo had learned to associate with flimflam artists—a thriving profession on the wide-open frontier.

Still sitting in his saddle, Ruck-a-Chucky gazed round at all four women. He had lost his leather cord somewhere, and his unrestrained hair, reeking of bear fat, was a wild black tangle.

"*Hijo de puta y chinga tu madre!*" he greeted the ladies in perfect Spanish, adding a string of high-falsetto giggles.

"What did he say?" a laughing Tammy asked Fargo.

Fargo slanted a knowing grin toward Snowshoe, who like Fargo knew some Spanish. The Modoc had no idea what he had just said. "Ah, basically, he said top of the morning to all you lovely ladies."

Ruck-a-Chucky swung down clumsily from his horse, almost losing his balance. But the man mountain recovered and effortlessly swept Fargo up into a crushing bear hug.

"What's on the spit?" Fargo greeted him as Yvette handed Ruck-a-Chucky a cup of coffee. He laced it with rotgut from the bottle in his coat pocket.

"Chucky brings bad news," the Modoc replied. "These prospectors . . . Running Antelope has called a meeting of the War Council. Very soon it will be the Moon When the Ponies Grow Fat. I think they will strike then, you bet your bucket!"

Fargo feared the same. Running Antelope, a local Nez Percé chief, was legally a ward of the American government now with no authority to wage war. But laws meant nothing if only one side respected them. Whites were trespassing on the restricted reservation, and their government was doing nothing to stop them.

"Happens what he says is true," Snowshoe muttered, "this region will run with white man's blood. The Nez Percés ain't a tribe to rile quick, but it's death to the devil when they paint for war."

Ruck-a-Chucky sneezed. The white shell in his "pierced" nose flew splashing into his coffee. His flood of silly giggles triggered laughter around the fire. But Fargo was also reminded of something.

"Chucky, why in hell are you still wearing that idiotic thing? You promised me you'd stop passing yourself off as a Nez Percé."

Ruck-a-Chucky shook his head as he fished the piece of dentin shell from his coffee. "Not on your tintype, mister! Chucky only said no more contracts. Can't take shell out yet. Too many whites he lied to."

"Running Antelope catches you," Fargo warned him, "he'll do the hurt dance on you."

"He is my wife's cousin," Ruck-a-Chucky said smugly.

Fargo knew Ruck-a-Chucky was a piss-poor "Indian

brave"—he'd learned the white man's greed and cunning instead of the traditional Modoc ways. But he was a passing shot with his Smith & Wesson repeating rifle, strong as an ox, and a brave man drunk or sober. Besides, this was an excellent defensive position if attacked in broad daylight.

"Chucky, me and Snowshoe got some business to tend to down near the river. Can I count on you to keep an eye on these ladies while we're gone?"

Ruck-a-Chucky ignited another explosion of mirth when he nodded vigorously and replied in his perfectly aped Texas twang: "I ain't never tasted bad whiskey nor seen an ugly woman."

Fargo borrowed tweezers from the twins so he and Snowshoe could dethorn their mounts' hooves before riding out. Thorns were a serious problem in mesquite country and in river growth like this wild profusion in Hell's Canyon. Left to fester, one thorn could kill both rider and mount.

While they worked, Fargo nodded toward the nearby corpse. "We'll wrap that up in my slicker."

"What, you mean this time you ain't staking the head down by their ford?"

A grim smile lifted one corner of Fargo's mouth. "No, but we may have better use for the entire body. My stallion won't tolerate hauling a dead man. If we tie it on your mule, will he haul it back to your camp?"

"Ignatius?" Snowshoe glanced proudly at his mule, grazing nearby with the Ovaro. Standing still, its uncut tail touched the ground.

"Hell, yes. He'd haul his own guts. That-'ere's a good animule. Oh, sure, he took the mustang fever once down in the San Saba River country, run off with a buncha wild broom-tails for a few weeks. Then he come trottin' home—ain't left since. A mule's a good lookout," Snowshoe adding, boasting. "And look at your pinto—lettin' Ignatius follow him around like a colt! Stallions tolerate mules like they will a gelding on account they don't compete for the mares. A mule's good eats, too."

They tacked their mounts and lashed the corpse to Ignatius. Then Fargo and Snowshoe swung into leather and headed down toward the river flats.

"All right, Fargo," Snowshoe said, "what's your grift this time? You ain't starvin' the vultures for nothin'. What you got planned for that-'ere body?"

Fargo's slitted eyes stayed in motion as the two men conversed, missing nothing. Marksmen could be hidden anywhere now.

"We're loading it into that skiff at your camp," he replied. "Then, after we detach that one-pounder, you're gonna float downriver in the skiff and wait for me to join you. I'll take Ignatius with me and ride. I'll make a map in the dirt, show you where to tie up and wait."

"A-huh."

A grin was already starting to divide the old trapper's walnut-wrinkled face. The arrival of Skye Fargo in any region always took the boredom out of life. "What you gonna be up to while this child's sittin' with the dead?"

"First I'll be removing the problem of the guard, or guards, outside their tunnel. Then I'm going to liberate their horses if I can. But I might need your help with that part, you old flint. You prefer to ride a mule because it matches your nature. But I've never seen a better man at handling horses."

Snowshoe spat amber, then beamed. "God's truth, ain't it? But, say . . . happens you take care o' the guards, why'n-'cha just wreck the tunnel?"

"Thought about it. But for one thing, they'll have another way in and out of wherever they're actually sheltered. Besides, that tunnel's most likely timber-reinforced."

"A-huh, that rings right. Be a bitch to rip them-'ere beams out, and it'd make such a racket with the first one, you'd just get yourself shot."

Fargo nodded. "That's why you're going to drift on downriver now with our quiet friend. I got a little show planned. Just one question. You know the Snake good—if we set that skiff adrift about two miles downriver from here, will we lose it for good?"

Snowshoe tugged at one of his pink-beribboned beard braids, envisioning the tortuous route of the river.

"Nah, it can prob'ly be retrieved. It'll hang up. 'Bout three, four miles down is where the boulders, gravel bars, and old beaver dams start. But wherever we haul it out is where we'll hafta cache it. *This* child ain't gonna portage that big skiff back overland."

"Fair enough. Long as I know where it is if I need it."

They had reached the thickly grown bank of the Snake. Fargo reined in and looked at his friend.

"This will be a rough piece of work today, Snowshoe. I won't blame you if you bow out. You don't owe those gals anything."

"Ah, pitch it t'hell, Fargo!"

Snowshoe swelled out his skinny chest. "A rough piece of work, my ass! Hell, *this* child learned his lore from Uncle Dick Wootton, down in the Raton Pass, when *you* was still a clabber-lipped pup. Why . . ."

Fargo shook his head, grinning, as the old trapper made his familiar brags. But the Trailsman kept his eyes in motion, his ears attuned to danger. He knew that Hell's Canyon truly belonged to devils—and that Skye Fargo was now number one on their list of the soon-to-be-damned.

12

"Boys, I shit thee not," Ace Ludlow swore, holding his hand up like a man taking a solemn oath. "You can't go gettin' icy boots over what happened to Zeke last night. Fargo's got lucky one time too many, and now the worm *will* turn."

"It ain't just Zeke, and you know it," Hoyt Jackson retorted. "First it was Fatty, then Ulrick. With Zeke, that's three killed. And what about Jack? Hell, Fargo blew half his ear off."

Ace was indeed fully aware of Jack Duran. Every man in the room was. He sat across the deal table from Ace, methodically stropping his razor. Since returning from last night's disastrous strike, he had spoken to no one. A huge purple bruise covered much of his jaw, and almost one entire side of his head was swathed in bloody bandages. He stared from glazed, unseeing eyes, hate starched deep into his pinched features.

"Hoyt, you'll get no argument from me," Ace said, "as to just how dangerous Fargo is. But a man has got to expect trouble before he can face it down. And Fargo don't expect trouble from Mattie."

This set off a ripple of mutters and curses among the rest of the men gathered inside the hidden cabin.

"We just leave it to your goddamn woman?" Hoyt exploded. He had small, dull eyes like a turtle, but right now they burned with rage.

"She *will* kill him, damnit!"

"When, Ace? Katy Christ, it's already the middle of the morning, and there ain't been no gunshots from the Seven Devils."

"She'll do it," Ace insisted. "She knows damn good and well her ass is deadmeat if she don't."

Ace reached down and pried up a few loose puncheon floorboards near the table. Then he grabbed the burning coal-oil lamp and held it over the opening.

"Glom that, chappies," he gloated. "And remember, it's equal shares."

A crawl space under the floor, but separate from the tunnel entrance nearby, was stuffed with sacks of stolen gold, weapons, valuable watches and rings, and other booty. Every man present stared longingly at it—except for Jack Duran. He continued to rotely strop his razor, lost in his own private dream of bloody revenge against Skye Fargo.

"Boys," Ace said, "you don't destroy the pasture just to get rid of the crabgrass. We got us a sweet thing here. All the matter with you is, you need a little poon, and then—"

Hoyt cursed, slamming a ham-sized fist into the table. "Need a little poon? What, like you got last night while me, Zeke, and Hoyt was facing down hot lead? We *got* poon! That's *our* tail Fargo is sittin' on! Let's just go get it. Now, all of us. No more jawing. Them's our women. Hell, doing it your way, Ace, is only getting us picked off."

A murmur of support bubbled through the close, stale-smelling air of the cabin. Ace could tell that Hoyt was a gnat's breath away from killing him and leading these angry, scared men in an all-out daylight attack.

"Hoyt, what you're suggesting just ain't a plan," he said. "It's just reckless and foolish. You need to leave the planning to your betters."

"You calling me stupid?"

The card games halted, and the men behind Hoyt cleared out of Ace's line of fire. Ludlow was a fast draw, and his special deadline trigger ensured an even quicker shot.

"Stupid? No," Ace replied, knowing that if he had to kill Hoyt he might as well turn the gun on himself right after. "Let's just say you ain't got the proper mentality to lead this gang. Not if you can't see the danger we all face and what we stand to lose."

He looked around at the rest.

"Boys, I know how you feel," he said. "But I been over it until I'm blue in the face: We don't dare do anything that gives away our hideout. A large group riding in or out will do just that. So I'll make you a deal. . . ."

Ace laid the boards back down. "The guard's been doubled outside, and the usual sentries are in place. We're safe for now. So we'll give Mattie the rest of this day to kill Fargo. Meantime, in case she doesn't, we'll put together another plan. Right now. One way or the other, we're finally settling accounts with that son of a bitch."

At Snowshoe's camp Fargo drew a dirt map to show his friend where he needed to bank in and tie up the skiff. If all went well, he should arrive before Fargo, given the speed of the current.

Then, crossing the Snake again on Snowshoe's ferry, Fargo began the dangerous ride south toward the Ludlow gang's hideout.

Snowshoe would need his mule for the escape, so Fargo led Ignatius by a line tied to his saddle horn. Fargo stuck to cover as much as possible, keeping a constant watch on the Ovaro's ears—often the first warning of danger. Anytime they pricked forward, Fargo halted to look and listen.

That's how he located the first guard.

Fargo and the Ovaro were still perhaps two hundred yards from the abrupt, twisting bend that marked the hidden corral and tunnel entrance. Just then the Ovaro alerted to a scent.

Fargo quietly dismounted and threw the reins forward, knowing that would hold his stallion in place. Ignatius loved horses, even stallions, and would stay at the Ovaro's side. Turning sideways to make less noise pushing through the brush, Fargo moved ahead cautiously. He wove his own path through brambles and scant-grown bushes just now recovering from the harsh winter.

Fargo had expected more security after his little visit yesterday. And now he spotted the new addition: Ace had stationed him in a tree overlooking the approach to the hidden cut bank: The same route Fargo used yesterday. A long Jennings rifle rested across the man's thighs.

Silence was essential now. Fargo doubled back around and crept up on the sentry from behind. He had perched on a fat limb about twenty feet up, craning his neck in every direction. Fargo realized now: Had he kept riding ten more yards forward, this killer would've had a plumb bead on him.

Fargo raised his right boot and slid the Arkansas Toothpick out of it. He faced a dilemma here, of sorts. Simply killing the man, outlaw or no, without giving him a chance to surrender was repugnant to Fargo. And killing him from ambush would make Fargo a murderer himself.

Yet, there was really no law hereabouts to surrender to. Even if Fargo took the man prisoner, what would he do with him? Nor was turning him loose, to continue killing and stealing, acceptable to Fargo. So there was really only one workable alternative: Fargo would peacefully announce his presence and let the man's criminal nature take its course.

"Howdy, up there!" Fargo called out pleasantly, holding the knife alongside his right thigh. "Got the time, stranger?"

Hearing the voice behind him almost startled the man out of the tree. He aimed a cross-shoulder glance at Fargo, cursed when he recognized him, and started to swing both himself and his rifle around.

"I ain't got you braced, so if you even *start* to aim that smoke pole at me," Fargo warned quickly in a no-nonsense tone, "I'll have to take great offense."

"Yeah? You'll take a .54-caliber pill, you stupid shit," the man assured him as he thumbed back the hammer to full-cock and started to aim his long Jennings.

Fargo made it one smooth, fast, continuous movement: He brought his right arm up and back, flexed, threw, released. The Arkansas Toothpick flew with blurring speed and lethal accuracy, slicing hard into the man's abdomen just below where he held his rifle. So hard, in fact, that the point buried itself at least five inches.

Fargo prayed the dropped rifle wouldn't discharge when it banged off the limb then slammed into the ground. It didn't. The man fell in the opposite direction, tumbling backward off his limb. He was already dead before he crashed into the bushes below like a sack of meal.

Fargo tugged his Arkansas Toothpick from the corpse, wiped the blade off on the man's trouser leg, then smashed the rifle against the tree. He returned to his stallion and Ignatius. He rode perhaps half the remaining distance to the cut bank.

Fargo dismounted in good cover and threw the reins forward again. He left his Henry in the saddle boot. The real cartridge session might still be coming. But Fargo intended to keep seizing targets of opportunity, like that guard just now, while working on breaking the will of the gang and scaring off its members.

First, however, he cut left to the swirling, splashing river and anxiously searched the bank behind him. There, almost out of sight from here, was good old Snowshoe, waiting beside the tied-off skiff with his Hawken rifle at the ready. *That old codger's dependable as the equinox,* Fargo thought as he waved him forward.

"The hell kept you?" Snowshoe groused when he arrived about ten minutes later. "Bust your leg in a badger hole?"

"Another jay in another tree. It was his call. Let's go take a squint around."

Fargo drew his Colt. Hugging the lip of the bank, they worked their way back downriver to the elbow bend where the cut bank was located. One man hugging each dirt wall, they followed it inland until they could peek around into the man-made chamber, hidden back under the cutaway riverbank.

One guard, a pox-scarred hard case toting a New Haven Arms magazine rifle. He was sitting on a keg near what looked like merely a tangled deadfall. Then Fargo studied it closer and realized it was also a natural screen for the tunnel entrance.

The makeshift corral's back wall was formed by the natural rise of the eroded bank, which curved over to form a shelter roof. It had been dug in a circle so the horses, if panicked, wouldn't dash themselves to death at the corners. Fargo peered over a corral gate of poles disguised by freshly cut brush. He spotted a roan, a coyote dun, several claybanks, and sorrels, including Jack Duran's.

With typical outlaw cruelty, the horses had all been left picketed on tight, restrictive tethers. The picket pins had been stamped in deep and covered with earth, thus they could be pulled up vertically, but not by a horse setting back or running on his rope. Several of the horses also had galled sides from tight cinches—no horse had it worse than an outlaw's mount.

The two men had seen enough. Fargo gave the high sign

and they moved back out to the natural part of the cut bank visible from the river.

"How we gonna skin this?" Snowshoe asked. "Likely, they'll hear any gunplay out here."

Fargo glanced around and selected a fist-sized rock. He never used his valuable handgun as a club.

"Nobody passes up fresh game or fowl in these parts," Fargo said, wedging himself into a narrow declivity in the dirt wall of the cut bank. "And you do good calls. Move down the bank about twenty yards, then hide in the brush and imitate a wild turkey."

Snowshoe bared his brown teeth in a wolf grin. A minute later, a convincing, warbling gobble rose up from the direction of the bank.

The bored guard wasted no time rising to the bait. Only moments after Snowshoe made the call, he came easing out of the cut bank, his eyes searching upriver toward the noise.

The second he eased past Fargo's position, the Trailsman beaned him a good one. The man grunted once, then dropped as if he'd been poleaxed. Fargo didn't conk him hard enough to kill him. Just hard enough that he might, after he fully recovered in a few days, contemplate the wisdom of his outlaw ways—at least, in this region.

Fargo tossed the man's magazine repeater out into the river. Then, while Snowshoe trotted back to join him again, Fargo dragged the unconscious guard aside, out of danger from trampling hoofs.

"Let's scatter the horses," he said as they both headed back toward the corral. "They may eventually round some of 'em back up or steal replacements. But they can't be killing prospectors or going after the women while they're busy scratching up more mounts."

"A-huh, but let's get it did fast. Happens Ace comes outside with that scattergun o' his 'n we're stew meat."

"That's a mighty consequential gun," Fargo agreed.

They threw the pole gate open. The horses, at the arrival of strangers, began to whinny and fight their tethers. Snowshoe went to work quickly before the racket rose loud enough to draw out the rest of the gang.

"Lookit," he said, pointing at a big claybank stallion rearing onto his hind legs, fighting the tight tether. "That-'ere's the master. Got a belly full o' bedsprings, ain't he?

Gentle him, we got the others. See how he's got his head low? That's when a horse is mean. Snub 'em high, sweet as a pup. . . ."

While he said all this, in a calm voice really meant for the stallion, Snowshoe advanced toward the rearing clay-bank. He removed his filthy bandanna and unrolled it. The moment the stallion's forelegs came back down, but his head was still up, Snowshoe leaped agilely forward.

Using the bandanna as a blind, he got the stallion to stand still long enough to press his mouth to its nostrils. The claybank accepted him after only a few breaths. As Snowshoe had predicted, the other horses also immediately submitted. The old ways, Fargo marveled.

They yanked out the pickets, detached the tethers and bridles, and led the horses out to the open bank.

"Point 'em south," Snowshoe said. "Good graze starts past the bottom of the canyon. Better off wild than with hard tails like Ace Ludlow."

Snowshoe bit the claybank's ear hard while Fargo, at almost the same moment, smacked it a loud one on the rump. The stallion was off at a run, the other horses following.

"All right," Fargo said, casting an anxious eye toward the interior of the cut bank. "We got to work fast, old son. Somebody's bound to give the hail to that guard sooner or later. When he don't answer, we'll be up against it."

Fargo hooked a thumb upriver. "You light a shuck back to that skiff. Make sure everything's set just like we planned it. Then shove it out into the current. Soon as she's adrift, go wait for me where I left our mounts."

Fargo described the spot, and Snowshoe hustled back to the skiff. Now came a tricky piece of timing for Fargo. In order to achieve the maximum punch from his plan, he had to make sure as many of the gang as possible came out into full view of the river—and in time to see that skiff drift by.

One thing would draw them out of the cut bank faster than a finger snap—the sight or smell of smoke. Any wildfire, in this tangled growth, could spell disaster for the gang holed up here. In truth, most of the growth was still too green to catch fire easily. But the men wouldn't think about that in the first confused moments of discovery.

Fargo had already selected a small bench of ground covered with old dead tuft grass and ground vines. It was in a spot where fire was unlikely to spread very far this early in the warm months, especially as the gang would be sure to smother it.

Still, he didn't like doing this. On the frontier, people caught deliberately firing the grass were shot like snakes, and with good reason.

But this bunch were far worse than snakes, he reminded himself.

They killed men in their sleep, stole the fruit of their hard labors, and doomed entire families to starvation and ruin. But that wasn't enough—they even lured innocent women into their rat hole to serve as degraded sex slaves. When they inevitably became pregnant or diseased, they'd be put down like sick animals.

Even as he ruminated, however, Fargo kept a close eye on the cut bank as well as Snowshoe's progress. He knew about how long it would take Snowshoe to hoof it back to the skiff; also how long it would take the skiff, at about four miles per hour, to drift abreast of the cut bank.

While he waited and kept watch, Fargo opened the drawstring possibles bag on his belt. He had about half a dozen phosphors, wrapped in a piece of oilskin to keep them dry. But when he pulled the matches out, he felt his heart sink like a stone.

Somehow, the oilskin had worked open and the phosphors were all dampened beyond use. Fargo cursed his own carelessness for not examining them before this. It looked like he could kiss his clever plan good-bye, thanks to his greenhorn blunder.

He also had his flint and steel in his possibles bag. But that was too slow, compared to lucifers, to ever fire that grass in time to draw the men out here from cover before that skiff floated past. Just as it was too late to stop Snowshoe. Hell, might's well just use an ancient Indian fire drill and take hours.

"All right, then," he resolved aloud. "I'll just have to get 'er done with what I got."

Never had Fargo called on all his speed and expertise with the flint and fire steel as he did now. Willing himself calm, his hands steady as solid oak but swift and sure, he set to work.

Still keeping an eye on the cut bank, he took a big pinch of punk, fine fibers of decayed wood, from the bottom of his possibles bag and made a little bed of it in the grass. Then, focusing all his skill, he started making slicing blows with the oval-shaped steel against the small piece of flint.

Fargo put his back to the breeze, sheltering the delicate bed of punk. It was his only hope of success—unless it, too, had been dampened. Again and again a downward-directed shower of sparks was caught in the tiny fibers. Carefully controlling his breath, he blew on the smoldering punk until he had finally coaxed it into a small flame.

Next came more substantial materials, small sticks and dead grass. But now he could see the damned skiff, or at least the prow. It was already approaching the beginning of the river bend that had carved out the cut bank.

Cursing again, he ripped out more grass, tore up some dead vines, and laid them onto his fledgling fire. Best he could do now. If the wind blew it out or his kindling smothered it, Fargo knew those outlaws would never come out far enough in time to see the skiff. There *had* to be enough smoke to scare them out or this entire day would be written off as a bad job.

Fargo stood up, drawing his Colt and pointing it into the sky. He divided his attention between the gathering flames, beginning to snap and spark a bit, and the approaching skiff. When he dared wait no longer, he fired two shots in quick succession.

Then, trusting it all to whatever god ruled the frontier, Fargo started running toward the rendezvous point.

"I never said it was a perfect plan, boys," Ace Ludlow repeated to his tense and nervous men. "But it's better than riding off hog wild, raising big dust puffs and making more racket than Fourth of July."

Hoyt Jackson had calmed down somewhat. He nodded agreement.

"It's not a bad plan," he admitted. "There's eight of us left, you making nine. So us eight split up into four teams of two, ford the river at different spots, then assemble with you for a massed strike just after dark when they're eatin' supper. We tie and gag the women, 'cept for Mattie. Bring 'em back here same way we left, each team with one woman and you with Mattie. That about it, Ace?"

"Chapter and verse," Ace said. "Except you left out the best part—killing Fargo and that old strip of jerky that's siding him. Don't forget, it was the old geezer who shot Zeke."

Ace had most of the men calmed down somewhat. But he sent another worried glance at Jack Duran.

Still, the man had said nothing, had hardly moved except to strop his razor. His hatred of Skye Fargo had evidently reduced him to a paralyzing stupefaction.

"Jack?" Ace coaxed his longtime friend and ally in crime. "Whatcha think of the plan?"

No response. Just *sswiit, sswiit, sswiit* . . . by now his cutthroat razor was honed so sharp it was taking slivers off the leather strop.

"Jack?" Ace coaxed again. "You in, buddy?"

Sswiit, sswiit, sswiit . . . Duran's thin lips had curled back off his teeth. Perhaps, Ace thought, he was envisioning Skye Fargo screaming under the blade, begging for mercy, admitting just who was the better man as his skin curled off like wood shavings.

By now Duran's odd behavior was becoming hard to just ignore. Despite his obvious rage, and the danger he always represented, he cut a comic figure with his bandage-swathed head and creased jaw. Only fear of his violent nature held the men's tongues in check.

Finally, however, Hoyt got fed up with it.

"Hell, Jack," he said, "snap out of it! No need to get so wrathy. Just grow your hair long, and that ugly-ass, ruint ear of yours won't even show."

Damn you, Hoyt, put a sock in it, Ace thought. Only Ace, who knew Duran well, had noticed how his jaw tightened at Hoyt's remark. That was always a prelude to trouble.

"Besides," tossed in Harley Peatross, who had joined Ace's gang a month ago, "it ain't exactly like you was a baby-blue pretty boy or anything, Jack, before you lost that ear. What's one more ding in a smashed pan?"

Ace watched Duran's knuckles turn white around the ivory handle of his razor and knew he was on the feather edge of erupting. Ace opened his mouth to warn the others, but just then Peatross rashly added:

"Hoyt, growing his hair out won't help Jack none. Can't you see he's going bald, you muttonhead? 'Pears to me Fargo has earmarked him for life, and—*Christ*!"

Jack Duran almost literally exploded. Roaring deep from his chest like an enraged grizzly, he launched himself from the chair, toppling it hard, and across the table at Peatross. Only Hoyt's powerful bear hug prevented Duran from slicing Peatross's throat open like soft cheese.

Just then, muffled but loud, came two shots from the river.

"Fargo!" Duran exclaimed, leaping for his Sharps Big Fifty.

"Don't run off half-cocked, boys," Ace ordered, lifting the trapdoor that led to the tunnel. "Pete!" he shouted at the top of his lungs. "Pete, what's going on?"

No reply.

"Let's go!" Ace ordered, palming the wheel of his Paterson Colt. Then he grabbed his loaded double-ten. "Get heeled and follow me. But watch for a trap."

Ace moved at a cautious crouch through the damp, cold tunnel. Soon he could see daylight at the entrance through the tangle of cover, and sensed something was wrong.

Ace poked his head out cautiously, then fired off a string of curses. He and his men streamed out into the corral.

"God-*damn* that Fargo, he's sprung our horses! Harley, check Pete—is he dead?"

"Nah, but from the looks of his head, he'll wish he was when he comes sassy. I'd wager Fargo killed Brubaker. I don't see him in the tree or—Christ! Look over there, boss!"

Harley pointed north, where fleeing buckskins and a flat-brimmed hat could be seen in glimpses through the growth.

"Jack! Put daylight through him with that Big Fifty!" Ace shouted.

But Duran was one step ahead of his boss. His huge Sharps was already loaded. He cocked it, threw it into his shoulder, and drew a bead on his man.

Fargo wasn't making it easy. Knowing his back was a tempting target, he bobbed and wove as he ran.

The Big Fifty bucked hard, roaring and coughing a great cloud of blue smoke. The hat flew off Fargo's head. He amazed every man watching when, without once breaking stride, he reached up and caught it in midair. The next second, he was gone from view entirely.

"*Bas*-tard!" Duran screamed, so frustrated he was close to tears.

But it was time for Fargo's little show.

"Holy shit!" Hoyt Jackson roared out. He pointed just behind them and closer to the river. A dark plume of smoke rose up.

"Fargo's fired the grass!" Ace said. "C'mon, boys, let's smother it quick before it spreads toward the cabin."

Ace topped the crest of the bank at a full run, starting to pull off his jacket. Then, stumbling to a full stop, he saw what was just now coming out of the bend in the river—a big wooden skiff.

What the hell?

Ace felt ice water replace the blood in his veins. The rest of the men saw him staring and followed his horrified gaze.

"Zeke?" Hoyt Jackson said tonelessly, the color ebbing from his blunt face. "*Zeke?*"

"Great jumpin' Judas!" Harley Peatross said, eyes wide as silver dollars.

Zeke Barlow appeared to be sitting comfortably on the aft thwart, a board seat, of the skiff. One chalk-white hand lay on the tiller, the other held a fishing pole, its line dangling into the water!

There was even a clay pipe stuck between his teeth. And his glass-button eyes, Jack Duran noticed with stomach-churning horror and revulsion, were staring up toward the living. Wide open. As if mocking them, inviting them to come join him on his final journey down the River Styx. Straight to hell in a skiff . . .

I cannot abide a staring corpse.

Duran fell to his knees, retching. The rest of the men stood petrified, ignoring the snapping flames. They stared in ghastly fascination as Zeke Barlow floated lazily past like a piece of driftwood—fishing, smoking, cheerfully oblivious to the blue cloud of flies buzzing around his exposed entrails.

13

The sun was westering and starting to lose its meager warmth by the time Fargo and Snowshoe returned to the twin camps on the mountain slope.

With no danger of pursuers, thanks to their release of the gang's horses, the ride back had been easy on their mounts. Knowing graze was scarce back on the slopes, the two men had let Ignatius and the Ovaro stop often to nibble at the tender buds and shoots so plentiful in a river-bottom woods just after first snowmelt.

They stripped the tack from their mounts and turned them out with the team horses and the Appaloosa. By now the dwindling graze had forced them to the highest part of the meadow, well above the camps. Even in daylight hours, Fargo knew, it was unwise to keep them so far from camp.

"They're cutting off the last of it," Fargo remarked, hooking a thumb back toward their mounts as the two friends walked down the slope, lugging their tack and weapons.

"That's a fack," Snowshoe replied, knowing more was coming and waiting to hear it.

"So to hell with retrieving that skiff. I think we should start pushing north toward Fort Walla Walla tomorrow. Over land."

"Got to be did sooner or later," Snowshoe agreed.

"I ain't saying I expect a stroll through the roses. But we've killed four of Ludlow's men now, and left most of the others wetting their pants today after that skiff floated by. You old reprobate, that was a fine touch with the pipe."

"A-huh, absodamnlutely. Never smoked it, anyhow. A

whore in Omaha give it to me, said the man what owned it was lynched, so it was juju."

Another spasm of laughter shook Snowshoe's wiry frame. The two men had been able to watch, from good cover, when Jack Duran upchucked.

"I *think*," Fargo said cautiously, "that we've snapped the back of the gang. Outlaws ain't the kind to keep pushing when a thing won't move. Too much sweat in it. But the snake's still got fangs. For Duran, at least, all this is personal. He'll stick until me and him hug."

"A-huh, that shines. And goin' on what this child has heerd about Ace Ludlow, he'll mebbe stick, too, seein' this as sorter a blood grudge. Both them no 'count sons-a-bitches was happy as pigs in shit until you come along. Boy, they mean to put a double-hog-tie hurtin' on you."

" 'Course, if we push north tomorrow," Fargo added as if Snowshoe had not spoken, "that means one of us'll have to scout ahead most of the time. Not only for a passable route, but for water and new campsites with graze. And there's plenty of good ambush country around here."

"A-huh. Don't it frost ya?"

Snowshoe loosed a dark streamer onto the ground.

"Ahh, ever dang place we dust our hocks to gets ruint by cussed syphillization, don't it?" Snowshoe lamented. "Use to was, this area was middling peaceful. Now it's maggot-riddled with these killers, and greedy trespassers who cash in and get out, no love or respect for the place. Plague take 'em!"

"There's a few good ones in the mix," Fargo said.

"Yeah? Well piss on them, too," Snowshoe growled, too ornery to be reasonable. "Mebbe this child will drift back east to the Plains. A man can still shoot buff and live on hump. Ain't near as pretty, though. This here is nice country."

It was that, Fargo agreed, gazing round at the late-afternoon, golden-hazed panorama of sky, mountains, canyon, and river. It reminded him of a simple question the Trailsman often asked himself to fill a solitary hour in some rustic camp: Just *who* "owns" the empty land of the American West?

If God made it, like the Bible-thumpers claimed, then

exactly when the hell did He deed it over to the railroad plutocrats, miners, cattle barons, and that special breed of parasites Fargo called the New York Land Hunters? Yet these were the very forces now telling free men where they could or could not graze their horses or spread their blankets.

By now the two weary men were almost at the women's camp. All the gals, except Mattie, Fargo noticed, ran out to meet them, Ruck-a-Chucky leading the way.

At first, however, with so many pretty women flocking toward them, neither man much noticed their Indian friend. The Papenhagen twins were especially eye-catching. They both wore snug blue cotton dresses, and they jiggled impressively as they ran. Their long blond hair streamed behind them, and their fair, fresh-scrubbed Scandinavian cheekbones glowed like an angel's halo.

"Hot *damn*," Snowshoe muttered to Fargo. "Grab your ankles, cupcakes, we're gonna doggy dance."

Fargo snickered at the dirty old man. Ruck-a-Chucky's silly high-falsetto giggles finally caught Fargo's attention.

"Bless my buttons!" the Modoc shouted in a joyful roar. "Both Chucky's friends came back, you betcher bucket!"

But neither man heard this. At first sight of him, they had both collapsed onto the ground, howling with mirth.

"Stop that, you yahoos!" Tammy snapped. "He looks real nice."

"God's blood, Chucky!" Snowshoe managed, sputtering tobacco juice all over the new pink ribbons in his long beard braids. "Old Snowshoe might's well die right now, he's finally seed it all."

While the two men were gone, the women had transformed Ruck-a-Chucky into a London dandy, or at least his bird's-nest hair. The unruly mess had been washed, then slicked down and made to shine with perfumed Macassar oil. Then they had rolled it into curl papers and shaped it into a high pompadour.

"That-'ere's what you'd get," Snowshoe told Fargo, "when you breed a French gal-boy with a three-hunnert-pound go-rilla."

"We heard shootin' again, down yonder by the river and south from here," Tammy said. "We was scared for you."

"We" evidently meant Tammy and Yvette, for each had

taken one of his arms and joined him. It surprised Fargo, because earlier both women had been at daggers drawn with each other.

Yvette read this thought in his face and, sending him a low-lidded smile, explained.

"Tammy and I have made an agreement. You are plenty of man for both of us. And since you obviously are not a one-woman man, and will soon be drifting on with the wind, we want to enjoy you while we can. Why spoil it for everyone, *non*?"

Fargo felt a grin tugging at his lips. "*Oui, oui, oui*," he agreed.

Nor was salty old Snowshoe being denied a warrior's homecoming. The twins, who seemed to have more than a granddaughterly interest in him, had already flocked to their favorite. They were untying his ribbons and fussing with his braids.

"Was it awfully dangerous, Snowshoe?"

"Ahh, it was pee doodlcs!" He thrust out his chest. "Some days you're the swatter, some days you're the fly. Today, me and my favorite turd here done the swattin'."

"Any trouble up here?" Fargo asked Ruck-a-Chucky.

"No trouble. But Chucky had a visitor, you bet. Little Horse, who is in my wife's clan. He refused food, a thing Chucky has never seen him do. He would not admit it, for he does not trust me, but he is fasting."

Fargo nodded, taking his point even though Ruck-a-Chucky was holding back so as not to alarm the women. Fasting was a widespread Indian custom before engaging in a battle campaign. Time was running short for whiteskins in this area.

"We'll be moving north tomorrow," Fargo told them, "and none too soon, looks like."

They had reached the camp. Mattie had emerged from the celerity wagon in time to hear Fargo's announcement. Oddly, he noticed, this time she raised no objections.

And, once again, her hands were tucked out of sight inside her shawl.

With Fargo and Snowshoe back, Ruck-a-Chucky was free to ride down to the river and check one of his setlines. He returned with a fat string of trout for supper.

"That-'ere damn redskin needs a pocket compass to find his own peeder," Snowshoe remarked to Fargo around a mouthful of steaming and savory baked trout. "But he's got sand in a shootin' scrape, and ain't nobody scrounges up eats better. Good man to take north with us."

"Already asked him," Fargo replied. "Says he'll go. He's afraid to go back to California anyhow—says his wife will geld him for being gone so long."

"So he's stayin' away even longer? There's Injin logic for ya."

Fargo watched Mattie, one hand hidden in her shawl, pick up the coffeepot and start around the campfire, filling cups. Here we go again, Fargo thought. That gal's a one-trick pony.

"Tomorrow, at first light," he told Snowshoe, "you and me are riding down to your camp. You can get what you need, and we'll drag that one-pounder back."

Snowshoe bared tobacco-stained teeth. "The hell you up to now, boy?"

"Never hurts to have a small cannon in your hip pocket. Ace has got a specialty weapon, so we need one to counter it."

Mattie edged closer, topping cups. Snowshoe nodded toward the canyon bottom, wrapped in a cloak of darkness now.

"Think they'll hit us tonight?"

"We prob'ly bought ourselves a one-night breather. But don't forget, they had a few sentries out, so they're not completely without horses. They could still pull something, so we best be ready."

"This child's always ready, hoss. That's why he's still sassy."

In a clumsy repeat of earlier in the day, Mattie moved behind Fargo and seemed to pause needlessly long, as if trying to decide something. A moment later, however, she poured his coffee from a trembling hand.

"Mattie," Fargo remarked mildly, "I notice you've made no complaint about pushing on tomorrow. You finally giving up on Chandlerville?"

Her answer surprised him. "I don't know what to believe anymore . . . Skye. I think it's best to let you take charge."

The submissive tone was new, and this was the first time

Mattie had ever used his front name. To cap the climax, she deliberately let her hair tickle Fargo's cheek as she stood back up and moved on. Snowshoe noticed this.

"You piker, Fargo," he muttered. "Looks like you're 'bout to bag your third quail. You leave me have first crack at them 'ere twins, hear?"

Fargo wasn't at all sure of Mattie's motives. Only three days now since he had "imposed himself" on the women, to use her phrase. True, a woman's physical wanting could be as powerful as a man's, as Fargo knew firsthand. But the sea change in her attitude was too sudden.

"We'll spell off on guard like last night," he told Snowshoe. "Ruck-a-Chucky will sleep next to the conveyance. Bring Ignatius in damn close, Snowshoe. The gang might try turnabout on us."

Fargo and Snowshoe first brought the team horses and Ruck-a-Chuck's Appaloosa in and hobbled them close to the women's camp. Snowshoe was standing first watch, so Fargo, taking no chances tonight, staked the Ovaro to his saddle horn and used the saddle for a pillow.

He couldn't help wondering, as he kicked off his boots and unbuckled his thick leather gunbelt, whose "turn" it was to wake him up tonight—Tammy or Yvette? Or maybe, now that they had an arrangement, both, in shifts? Hell, he had to get *some* sleep.

However, he didn't even have to wait until he nodded off to find out who was visiting him first tonight.

"Skye?" a female voice whispered even as he was settling in. "Still awake?"

Fargo's eyes snapped open, and Mattie Everett was on her knees beside his bedroll. The buttery moonlight revealed that her shirtwaist was unbuttoned despite the chill, baring a set of firm, nicely conical breasts.

"I have the same needs as the other girls," she told him, her voice husky with lust—or a good imitation of it, he thought.

But before Fargo could even react, she'd pushed her pliant bosom right into his face. Fargo smelled her lilac cologne, felt a chewy, spearmint-tasting nipple poke insistently into his greedy mouth.

Mattie made hungry mewling sounds as Fargo licked her nipples stiffer than the cold already had them. He popped open another button, his tongue tracing a hot line down across the gently rounded stomach.

"Jesus, honey, you taste might—"

Fargo's voice trailed off like the end of a song when he felt cold steel kiss his left temple. He opened his eyes. Mattie held the Colt Navy to his head.

"Damn, girl," he remarked, "you *do* know how to dampen a man's fire."

"And *you* know how to ignite a woman's," she replied, still breathing heavily. "I was faking when I started."

"You could always kill me *after* we do it," he suggested, still very much aware of the gun muzzle pressed to his head.

"Sorry, nice try. That part would be nice, all right. You're a powerfully virile and handsome man. But I'd never have the will to pull this trigger after being taken by you. I'd want more, and still more. A man like you just keeps stoking a woman's appetite."

"Jesus," Fargo said, instantly aroused again. "Mattie Everett, you *are* a hot little firecracker, are'n'cha? Darlin', you got my word—you just go ahead and do me, and then I'll shoot my*self*."

"Stop it! This isn't funny. Don't you understand, I'm going to kill you!"

"Seems to me, all you're doing is battin' your gums about it. You gonna go to church or stay home?"

He watched a desperate determination harden her pretty, worry-seamed face. Fargo couldn't see her finger on the trigger, but he could feel how the hand holding the gun was trembling violently.

"I'm sorry, Skye," she faltered out, "but I just *have* to."

However, the tearful catch in her voice gave way to a sudden collapse of Mattie's will. Sobbing miserably, she threw the Colt Navy aside and clung to Fargo.

"Oh, Skye, please forgive me! *What* did I almost do? I'll most likely be raped and killed, my family destroyed. But I just can't do it. It's bad enough what I almost did to those poor girls."

Fargo felt her bare breasts prodding him, hot and insistent. He wrapped her snugly in the blanket with him.

"Just what the hell has Ace Ludlow got on you, Mattie?"

"Plenty," she confessed. "When I was sixteen, my father caught me . . . being ardent with the young man he'd hired as a footman. We were only kissing and, well, fondling a little. But . . . well . . ."

"Your daddy," Fargo supplied, "threw an aces-high shit fit, right? Fired the footman, called you a hussy?"

"Called me far worse than that. He's a Calvinist preacher. Believes we're all sinners in the hands of an angry God. We had a terrible row; I ran away. I was literally destitute, starving. Ace Ludlow came along and 'rescued' me. At first he was so nice, almost like the loving big brother I never had."

"Yeah," Fargo said dryly, lightly tracing Mattie's bullet-hard nipples with his thumbs, "that's usually how they start."

"He saw right away that I could be invaluable to his criminal pursuits. He took me with him to states like Indiana, Ohio, Michigan, where there are lots of gullible small-town merchants and bankers vulnerable to sneak thieves. He used me as a decoy while he stole the money and goods. Eventually, though, he worked up to bigger game—express coaches out West. I was always the 'lady in distress' in a buggy with a broken axle."

"And finally," Fargo took over for her, "Ace killed a federal guard. And you're the 'unknown female accomplice' who's also wanted for murder in Texas?"

She nodded, blinking back tears. "I tried to break free of him, Skye, but he swears he'll kill me if I defy him. And he blackmails me. Despite my fight with my father, I don't want to see him and my mother ruined. And that's exactly what Ace will do by exposing me to the authorities."

"You do what I tell you," Fargo assured her, "and Ace Ludlow will *never* hurt you again. And if I have my way, he won't be exposing anybody—not from hell, he won't."

"I'm sure you're a formidable foe. But Ace and his good friend Jack Duran are like cockroaches—you can scare them away, but they're hard to kill. He'll survive, he always has, and he *will* expose me. I'll just have to take my punishment."

She sighed at the pleasure radiating from her aroused nipples as he circled them. "Skye?"

"Hmm?"

"Assuming I survive this, and Ace does expose me . . . will they hang me?"

"Hang a *woman* in Texas? Not even if you defiled the grave of Steve Austin. There's things the code just won't allow."

"They'll send me to prison, though, won't they? My family will still be ruined."

"It's hard to say what would happen to you. From what I hear, and read now and then in a crapsheet, law tends to go easier on a woman who's under a man's sway out of fear. Hell, he corrupted you young. You feared for your family and your own life—that ought to matter. How much it matters depends on the judge and how his digestion is on the day he passes sentence. But listen, Mattie . . ."

Her eyes were downcast in shame. Fargo tipped her chin up until they were gazing at each other.

"Ace Ludlow," he assured her, "may *think* he's ten inches taller than God. He's got you buffaloed, that's for sure. But the truth is, he's only a cowardly, murdering pig who pushes women around and kills defenseless men in their sleep."

She was so close, her full, moist rosebud lips so inviting. Fargo couldn't resist. He kissed her, their tongues hungrily exploring each other's mouths like probing fingers.

"My advice," he continued when they came up for air, "is to stop fearing what hasn't happened yet. You seem pretty sure Ludlow will survive all this and then ruin you and your folks. But I got another outcome in mind for old Ace. And when he dies, your secret goes with him, right?"

Hope worked into her face. "Oh, if only! But he's a sick, sick man. And so is that ugly little ferret Duran. But, if only . . . you'd do that for me, Skye, after I . . . I almost . . ."

She trailed off, gazing at the Colt Navy she'd tossed beside the bedroll. "You *trusted* me! Trusted me not to kill you. You're so incredibly brave."

"Now, don't start gushing like Yvette."

Fargo, looking a little sheepish, fished a hand into one of the saddlebags near his head. When he opened his fist, Mattie saw bullets.

"Trust everyone," he told her, "but always cut the cards. I sneaked them out of the gun before I left this morning. I knew you wouldn't check it—women think guns work by magic. I didn't think you'd pull that trigger, no. That's why

I let it play out just now—so you could convince yourself you're not like Ace."

Fargo settled her over on top of him, hiked up her skirt, and fumbled his trousers open, releasing his straining manhood.

"That's about enough jawboning for now, don't you think? Why don't we just do what we gotta?"

"Oh, *yes*," she moaned as his massive organ opened and filled the elastic, velvet depths of her love tunnel. "Oh, *yess*, like that, *just* like that, Skye . . ."

Ace Ludlow, squatting on his rowels behind a slight fold in the moonlit terrain, tasted the bitter bile of blind rage as he watched his woman—*his* private stock of high-grade—bounce up and down on Skye goddamn son-of-a-bitch Fargo until hell wouldn't have it again.

With each gasping, keening climax, she drove the insanely jealous and possessive Ace closer to the breaking point. His right index finger, curled around the twin triggers of his double-ten, literally itched.

But there wasn't a thing he could do about it at the moment. He was too far away to kill the pair of them. And if he moved any closer, that crusty old geezer with the buff gun would spot him. After what happened to Zeke here last night, Ace had learned to respect that old man.

Ludlow had ridden one of the three remaining horses, the three that were gone when Fargo emptied the corral earlier, just to come here tonight and talk to Mattie, to find out why in hell she hadn't put the quietus on Fargo yet.

Now he knew why. He hadn't been able to approach Mattie's camp because some fat-assed Indian, with the damndest coif Ace had ever seen on a red Arab, had plunked himself right in front of the celerity wagon, repeating rifle to hand.

Ace had watched Mattie slip away and hurry upslope to Fargo's position, but he couldn't catch her in time.

However, she still had to go back to her camp. And though a gunshot was out of the question, Ace could feel the weight of the solid-steel frog-sticker on his belt. He'd gut her like a fish. Or maybe just strangle that soft, lily-white neck of hers until it snapped like a dead stick . . .

131

Not only was that high-toned bitch wantonly defying him, Ace stewed, she was also ruining all his big plans in the process. This entire region could have been his crime empire if only Mattie had not turned his sweet cake into dough. A criminal empire to rival any, with Ace as head honcho.

Mattie fired off another string of gasping, moaning climaxes.

"Is that lanky bastard a studhorse?" Ace growled to himself. Hell, he himself climbed on and off a woman in about three minutes. That son of a bitch Fargo had been pounding the saddle for damn near an hour.

Finally, Ace watched Mattie's shadowy outline rise as she buttoned up her shirtwaist. Then a red-hot burst of rage turned his blood to acid when he realized: Fargo was taking no chances after last night. He escorted Mattie back down the slope, his Henry rifle tucked under one arm.

For all his festering rage and hatred, Ace did not lose his cunning survival edge. He had no stomach for facing down the likes of Fargo. Christ, after that stunt Fargo pulled off earlier with the skiff, Ace would be lucky if he even had a gang left.

Reluctantly, he began retreating back down toward the river and his waiting horse. But the sight and sound of his woman and Fargo putting the horns on him had been seared into Ace's memory to haunt him for life.

And *both* of them, he vowed, were going to die mighty damn hard.

14

"That'll do 'er," Snowshoe called down from the roof of the celerity wagon. "She's snugged down tight as a ladybug's—"

"Ahem!" Fargo cut him off sharply. "Ladies in the parlor."

Snowshoe looked contrite. "Sorry, ladies," he called out. "This old stag ain't around females much, firgets to launder his talk."

Fargo had just finished tying a double-hitch knot in two ropes lashing the one-pounder securely to the sturdy, steel-reinforced roof, designed to withstand hard rollovers. They had ridden out at first light, letting Ignatius and the Ovaro share the easy load as they dragged the small cannon back.

"Tuck this in with it," Fargo said. "Then cover the whole thing with my mackinaw."

He handed up Tammy's powder flask and the large leather pouch filled with patches and one-ounce lead balls. He had left a supply with Tammy, too, so she could charge her flintlock musket.

Next Fargo hitched the horses into the traces and hooked up the tug chains. Then he tied Ignatius to the rear of the coach with a lead line.

"All right," he told the assembled women when all was ready. "Everybody's going to be fine if we just hold to good trail discipline. There'll likely be trouble, but we can handle it if everybody follows the rules."

Fargo pointed northwest.

"As the crow flies, Fort Walla Walla is actually well west of us. But we have to bear due north at first, tracking the Snake, because we have to detour the Blue Mountains just to our left. We might get lucky, find a piece of a wagon road here and there. But mostly we'll have to scratch out our own trail over rough terrain, which means a scout will be out almost constantly."

Fargo paused, taking a moment to look each woman in the eyes. He wanted them to know he was damn serious.

"I'll be riding out to scout the first leg. Snowshoe will drive the team. Ruck-a-Chucky will be riding rover, never out of sight. I want *all* of you inside the wagon unless we're camped for night or stopped for short spells when Snowshoe gives his say-so to stretch. You don't go *any*where— not even into the bushes to pee, hear?—unless Snowshoe or Chucky is with you."

"Feel free, ladies," Snowshoe called down, the picture of innocent chivalry, "to go offen as nature calls. Me 'n' Chucky don't mind the trouble; no need to bust a bladder."

"Mighty thoughtful of you," Fargo deadpanned. "Tammy, Mattie—keep your weapons handy, but be careful with them in that crowded coach. You, especially, Tammy—that musket's bigger than you are. Don't charge it until there's trouble. And remember what I told you?"

"Make sure not to panic and forget to pull the ramrod out before I fire."

Fargo nodded. "Good girl."

"*Only* good?" she pouted.

"Don't distract me," he ordered, adding a quick wink.

He looked at Mattie, trying to suppress a little grin of complicity with her. No one else in camp, except the gloating Snowshoe, knew that Fargo and Mattie had pitched a little hay last night. She held her Colt Navy, loaded this time.

"Keep that weapon at your side at all times until we've reached the fort," he repeated. "Even when you bathe or sleep. And don't forget: A handgun is only a short-range weapon. Don't get flustered and waste your shots too soon. Truth is, most folks are lucky if they can hit a man beyond forty feet with one shot. Once it's time to use it, point the gun at the center of your target and shoot. Don't waste time 'aiming' or you'll likely get shot."

Ruck-a-Chucky already sat the saddle of his Appaloosa, ready to raise dust. His pompadour had gotten squashed during the night. Now his hair looked like a helmet of shiny curls. Fargo handed him the Ovaro's reins to hold a moment.

"A word with you in private, Mattie?" he said.

The two of them stepped away from the others.

"Mattie," Fargo said, "there's danger enough for all you gals. But for you especially. Those other four, they're valuable to Ace's scum, all right, for obvious reasons. But judging from what you've told me, Ace Ludlow won't just let you defy him and ride off like he would the others."

"No. It will be the object of his existence to get vengeance against me. He'd follow me into hell to get it."

Fargo nodded. "So that means you assume he or his lickspittles are dogging you. Waiting, watching for a chance. *Never* get far from that wagon. And no 'feminine modesty.' You do nothing without one of us men at your side. Better us peeking than Ace's bunch. Promise?"

"Promise."

"You two gonna swap spit?" Snowshoe groused from the box of the conveyance, shaking a blacksnake whip at them impatiently. "Augh! Stir your stumps, it's time to open the ball!"

All along, the aim of Skye Fargo and that old twist siding him, Ace Ludlow realized, had been to unstring the gang's nerves. And the strategy had paid off in spades.

The death of the sentry Brubaker yesterday had left eight men, counting Ace. But three of them had collected their shares and lit out as soon as they were horsed again.

That left Ace, Jack Duran, and Hoyt Jackson from the original gang, along with Pete Helzer, the guard who was beaned while on duty in the corral, and Harley Peatross. Harley had notched a dozen kills back in Missouri and Arkansas, and Ace considered him a good gun hand.

Ace figured by now the damage was done. But by mid-morning, a fourth man had decided to hightail it.

"This ain't personal, Ace," Pete Helzer said. "You're a good boss and all. But Fargo coulda killed me yesterday. I've had my warning, and I'm heeding it. Soon's I collect my share, that is."

Encrusted blood still caked Pete's hair where Fargo had

struck him with the rock. Clearly he was still woozy from the blow. The man looked pale, unsteady on his feet, and his speech was slightly slurred.

"Set it to music," Ace snapped. "The tune's gettin' familiar. I'm just surprised you're the fourth to rabbit instead of the first. At least you got a reason. Them other three just lack spine."

Pete stood uncertainly in the middle of the smoky, stale-aired cabin, not sure how to handle this. He was heeled, but in no condition for gunplay. Besides, he wasn't stupid enough to pull against Ace and his quick-kill trigger.

But Ace wasn't pushing things to that point. He was a man driven by one need now: to see Fargo *and* Mattie die hard. Fargo for touching his private stock, Mattie for her defiance and disloyalty. So Ace would risk no confrontation that might get him killed before sating his great need.

"It's all right, Pete," he said, rising from the table and kneeling to pry some floor planks loose. "You earned a share, you'll get it. You're a good man to ride the river with."

After Pete had left, Ace stared round the table at Hoyt, Harley, and Jack.

"All right, boys, it's time to fish or cut bait. We can sit here and whine like sniveling bitches, or the four of us can finish this thing. At least those weak sisters who quit did a good job of stealing horses last night. That works out perfect because Fargo's pushing north this morning. Jack spied on them earlier, saw them getting ready. That means they're losing the high ground."

"But the plan we worked out yesterday called for—"

"Hoyt, plans ain't written in stone, they change. There's only four of us now. Jack said Fargo went on ahead when they moved out. That means he's scouting, marking a trail for the old coot driving. The fat Indian with the bird's-nest hair is riding guard."

Ace's hard-bitten, mud-colored eyes cut toward the nearest wall. His double-ten leaned against it, freshly loaded. Ace had hand-crimped the shells himself after packing them tight with centavos, small, thin Mexican coins he kept just for the gun.

"This is the chance we been waiting for," he resumed. "Hoyt, you and Harley are gonna kill the geezer and the redskin and grab the women, bring them back here. 'Bout the same time, me and Jack will ambush Fargo."

"Hell, I ain't no general," Hoyt said, "but I thought it was never smart to split your force?"

Ace smacked the table so hard the lantern leaped. "No, I'll tell you what ain't smart—always going by damn stupid rules. Hoyt, we gotta cut our coat according to our cloth. This is the best plan."

Duran, who had been silent to this point, startled the rest by suddenly speaking up.

"I'll gut him like a fish. Neck to nuts, Fargo. Neck to nuts."

Ace nodded. "Razor, bullet, it's all one to me. I don't care who does it. Just so the bastard's wick gets snuffed. That randy stallion's had himself a high old time priding it over our stock. Now he's getting one more mare to his bunch—a goddamn *night*mare."

Fargo liked to scout by tossing a wide loop. But mountain ranges hemmed in Hell's Canyon and the river flats on both sides of him.

It was ideal terrain for ambushers, and Fargo didn't like it. But that situation would ease once they cleared the Blue Mountains on their left, opening a route to the northwest. They'd have a little wheeling distance then.

Despite the remote desolation, Fargo was surprised at the increasing signs that this area was settling up. Only two hours after he set out ahead of the rest, leaving trail markers for Snowshoe, Fargo actually encountered an itinerant peddler. Monocled, crop-carrying, sporting a British accent, he led a mule packed with gimcracks to sell up north in Lewiston.

But Fargo spotted even more men and goods bound for Lewiston on a grander scale. Steamboats were still in short supply in the far West. However, a break in the bottom woods, below and left of him, showed Fargo a glimpse of a twenty-two-oar keelboat. Fifty-five feet long, it was propelled, as occasion warranted, by its oars, by setting poles thrust against the bottom, or by tow rope. At blessed intervals, a favoring wind filled the big square sail.

More ominously, Fargo later spotted a large group of Nez Percé warriors down on the river. They were traveling in their frail but agile boats made from buffalo hides stretched across a frame of green cottonwood. Fortunately, the braves weren't painted for battle.

But Fargo felt the time pressures as he cast an eye about the rugged, uneven terrain. Deep seams and scars, glacier-strewn rocks and boulders everywhere. He was playing hell even finding a trail. They'd be damn lucky to eke out fifteen miles a day, which meant they could still be trespassing on Nez Percé land when the war whoops sounded.

"Pile on the agony," he said cheerfully to the Ovaro as he reined in to let the stallion drink from a little seep inside a cluster of huge granite boulders.

While the Ovaro dipped his muzzle into the bracing water, Fargo kept to the cover of a boulder and studied his surroundings with a keen eye. He had no concrete reason for the sense of unease he felt, just common sense based on knowing how the criminal dregs tended to operate.

To his east, farther up the slopes, gama grass meadows were greening. Fargo hoped they continued because the team horses would require plenty of graze. He glanced west, toward the tangled heart of Hell's Canyon, and saw prospectors working a creek with sluice boxes.

It all looked peaceful enough. Nonetheless, Fargo stopped the Ovaro before he could drink his fill. He didn't want the stallion loggy in case of trouble. And trouble, Fargo had discovered even before he could grow a beard, never let him get lonely for long.

This time, as so often before, Fargo's first warning came from his alert pinto.

The Trailsman was approaching a long rock spine, ahead and to his left, when the Ovaro's head swung up. When the stallion started circling, with no command from his rider, Fargo quickly guessed what was happening.

The Ovaro's peripheral vision had likely glimpsed a human form he didn't recognize. If a horse could see, but not smell, strangers, it must circle into their odor. And when the Ovaro's quivering nostrils found the scent, his ears pricked in the direction of the source—behind the rock spine, waiting somewhat ahead.

Fargo nudged the riding thong from the hammer of his Colt, loosed the Henry in its boot. He let the Ovaro walk slowly forward for perhaps another fifty feet.

Fargo didn't need to rein in. He simply dropped the reins

and the pinto immediately halted. The thin, razor-backed spine lay directly to his left now, so close he could spit and hit it. Fargo simply sat his saddle for a minute or two, his trained ear listening.

And then he heard the sound he sought: A faint, metallic rattling noise a man wouldn't even notice unless he knew what it was: horses running their tongues over the bits, rattling the little iron rollers on the bridle bar. His ambushers should have thought to throw their bridles.

Now Fargo knew right where they were, and right what they planned: They were waiting just behind the far end of the spine, and intended to ventilate his back with lead the moment he popped into their view.

But, of course, they expected him to be unprepared and moving slowly. And Fargo had no intention of accommodating them. Not with Ace Ludlow's butcher gun and Jack Duran's Big Fifty to cope with at one time.

He patted the Ovaro's neck, calming him and signaling that a hard run was required. It was his horse's speed and endurance Fargo intended to rely on, at least for the moment. Turning back was not an option. By continuing north, he'd draw his ambushers with him and away from the women.

Fargo cocked his shooter and lowered his profile in the saddle. Then he took the reins in his left hand and thumped the Ovaro's sides with his boot heels. The stallion shot forward like a startled antelope, hooves throwing up divots of dirt.

It was because of moments like this that Fargo refused to ride a gelding. Like the Indians, he believed gelding weakened a horse. And now, as he streaked past the end of that rock spine already at a full gallop, Fargo was glad he held out for stallions.

There! In a flash, he spotted the surprised, confused faces of Ace Ludlow and Jack Duran.

Just as Fargo had figured, they were already in position to drop him. Duran had even taken up a prone position with the muzzle of his Sharps resting on cross-sticks. Probably intending, thought Fargo, to shoot the Ovaro. In this country, a man afoot was no man at all. Two horses Fargo hadn't seen before, no doubt stolen last night, were picketed well behind them.

"Hey, Jack, lend me half an ear!" a grinning Fargo sang out in a taunt as he and the Ovaro came charging past in a streak. "How 'bout some hot beans, boys?"

Accuracy was impossible, so Fargo simply emptied his Colt rapidly, sending out a wall of lead to cover his escape. He heard both men cursing as they rolled desperately for cover. But within moments they had hit leather and Fargo could hear them in hard pursuit.

Let them come after him; Fargo knew he'd taken that hand. Unless the Ovaro was tripped up by a rock or one of the many gopher holes in this area, those two killers were just pissing upwind. The Ovaro was smart as a cutting horse, brave as a cavalry charger, as swift as an Arabian barb.

But even now, as he opened out a lead and felt the stallion's heart pulsing against his legs, Fargo couldn't help wondering: Were these two the only ones left from the gang? Or were others behind them, terrorizing the women?

Snowshoe Hendee had been reading sign for nearly forty-five years, and he was the first one to tell you he could track a one-legged ant across granite. So it was child's play to read the trail markers Skye left for him.

At several places there was more than one path possible, such as giant heaps of scree to be detoured or steep rises that had to be circled either east or west. In each case, Fargo had scouted all the choices and marked the best one with little stacks of rocks or a sharpened stick poked into the ground.

"Snowshoe?"

Yvette poked her coronet-braided head out of the window below him on his left.

"How long before we can stop?"

Snowshoe's red-rimmed eyes lit up. In a heartbeat he had a foot poised to kick the brake forward.

" 'S'matter, cupcake, you gotta pee?" he asked hopefully.

"No, but we're going so slow, and it's so crowded and stuffy back here. We'd just like to stretch a bit."

Snowshoe scowled and spat amber. "Stretch a cat's tail," he muttered under his breath, disappointed. The team had been laboring in the traces for damn near four hours, with only a few pauses to let them blow. And in all that time, nary one of them cottontails needed to tinkle! They'll all wait until Fargo's driving, he fumed.

"Getcher head back inside," he snapped at the pretty Creole. "Don't bother me with such truck. And you gals close 'em-'ere dust curtains."

Ruck-a-Chucky was riding just behind the right rear wheel of the coach. That way he could watch both the trail behind and Snowshoe's blind side.

"You hear that just now, Chucky?" Snowshoe made his voice high like a whining female. " 'We're going so slow, and it's *so* crowded and stuffy back here.' Pitch it t'hell! Nuff to frost ya, ain't it, with us out here takin' the arrahs? I like lookin' at their titties, but gol*dang*, women is simple-minded and ungrateful little shits, ain't they?"

Chucky, a little unsteady on the hurricane deck, kicked his horse up to a trot, riding up beside Snowshoe.

"My wife?" he said, his moon face solemn and worried. "She is good with the knife. I think she—"

"Don't *even* start with that damn castratin' wife of yours," Snowshoe interrupted. "She sounds a mite teched, to this child. But then, look at the brain bonanza she's hitched her wagon to."

Chucky giggled, nodding enthusiastic agreement. "Ja, dot iss true, py golly!"

Snowshoe abruptly reined in the team, dropping the brake forward against the rims. The jingle of the tug chains fell silent. The puzzled old trapper gazed off toward a stand of jack pine on their left.

"Lookit," he told the Modoc, pointing. "Why, it's a pair of red long-handles. Nailed to a tree. Now ain't *that* a poser?"

Snowshoe studied the area all around them. Fairly open, not a very good ambush point. No cover nearby at all.

"Could be a fox play," he reasoned, tugging one of his beard braids. "But they's times when prospectors will do that to give away extry clothes. That-'ere pair looks prac'ly new."

As he aged, the winters bothered him more. Snowshoe gave in to temptation.

"Hell, won't take but a minute. Ride on over there, Chucky, and grab 'em, wouldja?"

"You betcher bucket!"

Ruck-a-Chucky wheeled his Appaloosa and kicked it up

to a trot. He was about fifteen feet from the tree when, quick as a finger snap, the earth swallowed him whole!

Pitfall, Snowshoe realized instantly, cursing himself for a greenhorn. He'd fallen for a trap.

To the right, and behind him, the bush-disguised cover of a second, smaller pit was thrown back. Hoyt Jackson and Harley Peatross leaped out.

Snowshoe heard something, snatched up his Hawken, and started to turn. But Hoyt Jackson's Volcanic rifle spoke its piece, and the slug knocked Snowshoe backwards off the box.

His head slammed into the iron tire and his body got hung up awkwardly, feet tangled in the traces, head lolling over the wheel.

"Good work, Hoyt!" Peatross congratulated him. "Quick, we'll drag the women out and search 'em for weapons. Then we'll finish off the Injin."

He braced one foot on the step plate and gripped the brass door handle, practically ripping the door off the hinges when he yanked it open.

"All right, bitches, get the hell—"

Mattie fired the Colt Navy point-blank. A neat hole appeared in Harley's forehead, surrounded by a sooty black peppering of powder burns. The collapsing body almost knocked Hoyt down.

Mattie swung the muzzle toward Hoyt, but he slammed a huge fist into her jaw, instantly stunning her. He seized her weapon and thrust it in his belt. Tammy was just starting to bring her musket up when Hoyt swore and snatched it from her.

"You just killed my pard," he told the still dazed Mattie, his small, dull eyes now hot with pent-up lust. "So you climb on out here and get them dainties off, missy. You'll be the first."

Snowshoe, unconscious and bleeding, loosed a low moan.

"Here, you old sack of guts," Hoyt sneered, leveling the musket on him. "This'll put you out of your misery."

Hoyt had little experience with muzzle-loaders and hadn't checked to see if Tammy had removed the ramrod yet. He fired, the breech exploded, and the ramrod came rocketing out of the ruptured barrel, taking much of Hoyt Jackson's head with it.

15

Skye Fargo had just begun to lead his two inept pursuers on a merry chase when he heard it: the distant, but still powerful, report of a musket.

Tammy's musket, almost surely. He had foreseen a possible strike on the women, but it would be Snowshoe and Ruck-a-Chucky's job to handle it. If Tammy had been forced into the shooting fray, something must have gone seriously wrong.

Fargo's hunters got nothing but his dust as he easily shook them off in a series of erosion seams. Then he pointed south and kicked the Ovaro up to a run.

When Fargo arrived, he surveyed the aftermath of the battle and got the story from the shaken but still game females. He realized things could have gone far worse for the defenders.

The women had already dragged the bodies off to one side and thrown brush over them. Now they were even mounting guard: Mattie with her Colt Navy, Tammy struggling to hold Snowshoe's big Hawken, Yvette handling Ruck-a-Chucky's rifle as if it were a sleeping snake. Tammy's destroyed musket lay in the grass next to the spoils of battle: a blood-spattered Volcanic rifle and a Remington revolver.

"Ruck-a-Chucky seems all right," Tammy reported. " 'Cept for his right ankle's twisted. And his horse has already climbed out of the trap. You'll have to help Ruck-a-Chucky out, though—we can't budge him, he weighs a ton It's Snowshoe who got hurt the worst."

In hushed tones, Tammy described the way he had fallen, his head striking the iron-rimmed wagon wheel. From the ragged sound of his breathing, Fargo feared he might have fractured his skull.

Hilda and Helga were already fussing over Snowshoe, mopping his brow and making sure he was warm. The old trapper lay sprawled on a blanket, his breath rapid and shallow.

"Let me have a look at him," a worried Fargo said, kneeling over his friend.

The two twins hurried off to get some water.

"Snowshoe," Fargo said, fighting back a lump in his throat, "can you hear me? We'll do our best to save you, old son. Hang on, you hear me?"

One of Snowshoe's eyes popped open. "Don't start sloppin' over on me, hoss, and don't hem me! That bullet was pissant caliber and hit a long way from my heart. Just creased my side. It was the goldang fall what knocked my lights out for a spell. No need of the gals knowin' that, though, uh?"

Fargo peeked under the blanket, then almost burst out laughing. Despite a good amount of dried surface blood, Snowshoe had a simple flesh wound hardly more serious than a bad scratch.

But the old reprobate saw the twins hurrying back, their pretty faces a mask of worry. Snowshoe closed his eye again.

"Skye, old friend," he groaned weakly. "Is that you, boy? It's all goin' . . . sorter dark like, Skye, old chum. If only a lonely, dyin' man could just have the comfortin' touch of a woman's breast right now. . . ."

The twins cried out in consternation and almost literally smothered the cunning old lecher in affection. Fargo stared in amazement, shaking his head—Snowshoe's hoary old head was now sandwiched between four lovely knockers. He aimed a wink at Fargo before groaning in apparent misery.

Fargo quipped, "It's the wheel you best worry about, ladies, if *his* head hit it."

Still shaking his head, he grabbed the rope off his saddle horn and took up the Appaloosa's bridle reins, leading it out to the pitfall. Even before Fargo arrived, he could hear Ruck-a-Chucky singing an Irish ballad.

When he peeked into the pitfall, the Modoc loosed a string of silly giggles. "Chucky likes it down here," he called up, flat on his back and nursing a bottle of Indian burner. "No wife."

"You and Snowshoe amount to a fine pair of 'frontiersmen,'" Fargo said as he threw one end of the rope down to his friend. "I find him wet-nursing, and you flat on your ass in a pitfall, drunk as the lords of Creation. Good thing them *helpless* women had you two he-bears to protect them, uh?"

"Ain't it the drizzling shits?" Ruck-a-Chucky agreed, giggling some more until a ripping belch interrupted him. He giggled at that, too.

"Jesus Christ, Fargo," the Trailsman muttered to himself, "maybe you *ought* to consider city living."

Practically herniating himself, Fargo hauled the big Indian up and took a quick look at his ankle. Some swelling, but no broken bone or hard sprain. Fargo wrapped it with a tight strip of buckskin. He helped Ruck-a-Chucky onto his horse and they returned to the others.

"There's still a few hours of daylight left," Fargo told them. "Despite the delay, we can still make it to the campsite I picked for tonight."

"Oh, but, Skye!" one of the twins exclaimed (Helga, Fargo realized, seeing the little freckle bridge on her nose). "We dare not move Snowshoe. He's at death's door."

"*Annnnhhhh!*" Snowshoe groaned, the sound muffled by female pulchritude.

Fargo had to bite his lip to keep from laughing at the old scutter.

"We have to, hon," he replied, "or the cold could kill him. There's a hard spring freeze coming tonight. I've felt it in the air all day. Temperature's been dropping steady and the wind's straight out of the north tonight, coming down off the Canadian ice."

"Is this campsite you have in mind sheltered, is that it?" Tammy asked. Her yellow gingham dress was flecked with blood.

"Even better," Fargo assured her. "This whole region is laced with underground thermal springs. When I was scouting, I listened for the rumble and found a good one under a few natural vents. There's fireplace heat pouring out of 'em night and day. We'll be warm as toast and won't need a fire."

Fargo glanced around. "We'd be fools to try and weather cold here. Not enough dead wood. And we're too far from the Plains to find any prairie coal," he said, meaning buffalo chips.

"Girls," he called over to the twins, "we'll need to tend to that old man's life-threatening wound before we leave. Best to strip him to the waist and scrub him good with lye soap and water."

Snowshoe's eyes popped open, alarmed, and he sat up spryly. "Damn my eyes! Was this child out?"

They pushed on, Skye and Ruck-a-Chucky flanking the wagon, Snowshoe back on the box driving after the twins cleaned and dressed his wound. About an hour after they set out, Fargo spotted the same large, pine-log structure he had passed earlier. It occupied a bluff, down in the canyon at the river's edge. It was a Nez Percé communal dwelling that housed several extended families.

Ruck-a-Chucky had already thrown away the shell in his nose when he realized the Nez Percé war drums were finally throbbing. Now, once again, the king of frontier scavengers came through for them.

He rode down to visit the communal house, taking a supply of coffee and good tobacco. He was able to barter for some dried fish and fruit, nuts, and a few flat cakes of unleavened wheat. Meager rations for eight stomachs, but Fargo figured it would tide them until he could tag some game.

But right now, with Ace Ludlow and Jack Duran on the prowl, Fargo had bigger game on his mind. Which was why he again took Mattie aside once they had camped at the thermal spring.

"Hell of a bruise that pig put on you," Fargo said.

Even in the fading light of day, he could see the huge purple mass covering her jaw.

"I've been hit harder by Ace," she admitted. "Besides, Tammy's old flintlock got revenge for me."

"You held up good today, Mattie," he added. "All you ladies did. Now two more of Ace's dirt workers are feeding worms. But don't forget, Ace and Jack Duran are still alive and most likely dogging us."

"Forget? Skye, it'd be easier to forget a tumor. At least a tumor only destroys you, not your family."

"He's a giant in your mind, unstoppable, and I understand that," Fargo said. "To me, though, he's just one more rabid cur that needs to be cut down before he bites again."

Mattie glanced around them in the rapidly gathering chill, pulling her shawl around her tighter. The north wind suddenly gusted to a mournful shriek. The cold Arctic air cut like a knife.

"From your lips to God's ears, Skye. I've lived in fear of him for fifteen years now. It's hard to believe I'll ever be free of him."

Mattie woke up in the hours just before dawn, her bladder aching insistently.

Outside her cozy-warm blankets, the icy wind howled like some crazy spirit. *Why* do women have to pee so much more often than men, she fretted. It felt so nice and steamy warm here, lying on heated ground near the thermal vent.

She poked her head up and glanced around. The rest were slumbering peacefully, lulled by the wonderful heat radiating up into their bedrolls. One of the men, she wasn't sure which in the darkness, was on guard. She could see his form perhaps fifty feet away, huddling over a vent for warmth.

Mattie glanced to her left, toward a brush-screened hollow. The girls had used it to do their business earlier.

She knew she should get the guard. But it was embarrassing to ask a man to watch you pee. And if that was poor Ruck-a-Chucky on duty, she'd be forcing him to walk on his hurt ankle. It seemed silly to risk waking everybody up when she could just dash over there and get it done.

Ace *hates* cold, she reminded herself. He wouldn't be lurking out there in the middle of a freeze.

She was already dressed except for her shoes, which she buttoned on now. Mattie wrapped a blanket around her and headed quickly toward the brushy hollow, shivering in the frigid wind.

She made it all the way to the first line of brush before she realized she'd forgotten to bring her weapon.

Skye's words prodded at her memory: *Never part with that Colt.*

"Oh, botheration," she whispered, irritated at herself.

She turned to go get it. Again the wind gusted, blistering cold.

Oh, this was silly! She'd freeze her hind end off going back for the gun. She was already here now, anyway.

Mattie hurried into the tangled cover, wanting only to return to her warm blankets.

Ace Ludlow had never been so damn miserably cold in all his thirty-five, hardscrabble years.

Neither had he ever paid much attention to learning the warning signs of nature, and this late freeze had caught him flat-footed.

He and Duran were camped in the bottom woods about twenty minutes ride from here. After today's taunt from Fargo, Duran had thrown a rage fit and beat his stolen horse half-senseless with the stock of his Big Fifty. Now he was resting up for the next attempt on Fargo's life.

Ace, however, had been unable to sleep. He couldn't stop stewing on Mattie and how much that two-timing, backstabbing bitch had cost him. He had spent years shaping and molding her to the outlaw life. But she was just a mushy-headed do-gooder after all, like her preacher old man. And her treachery had cost Ace his empire.

So he had slipped into the brush-filled hollow after dark and begun a long, boring, blue-ass cold vigil, hoping against hope that he'd get his chance to show her what happened when you cross Ace Goddamn Ludlow, girlie.

But no soap. The hours dragged by like aeons, the temperature plummeted, and all Ace had for his trouble was an even more intense need to feel the heat *whoosh* out of Mattie Everett as his cold steel frog-sticker punctured her vitals.

God*damn* her! She was Ace's private stock, yet she had willingly spread her legs for Fargo. Ace had watched, listened, while Fargo played Mattie like an instrument, coaxing high notes and harmonious chords out of her that Ace had never even heard before. Nobody gelded Ace Ludlow like that and lived to tell it. First he would kill Mattie, then Fargo.

Finally, when his manhood had disappeared up inside his stomach and he couldn't stop shivering, Ace decided to give it up for tonight. That's when he saw a shadowy form emerge out of the night like a wraith.

His pulse quickened when the figure passed through a moonbeam and he recognized the auburn tint of Mattie's hair.

Ace's thin, cruel lips formed a jagged slash as he grinned at this unexpected turn of events. Good old modest Mattie, sneaking out to take a whiz. Yeah, *that's* the gait, sugar, come to papa . . .

She was almost close enough now, so close he could just about reach out and clamp a hand over her mouth. Then slowly, inch by agonizing inch, he would force cold steel into her entrails. And once the blade was deep, he'd be sure to give it the Spanish twist so it hurt even mor—

"Mattie?"

Ace, on the verge of seizing her, started violently when Fargo's voice interrupted him. It came from the edge of the trees.

"Yes, it's me, Skye. Nature calls."

"I know, hon, but you know the rules."

"Sorry. Almost done."

"I'm waiting right here for you. Hurry it up. And next time, you take company along, hear?"

"Yessir, General Fargo! Br-r-rr! It's freezing."

Ace was trembling with rage and frustration now, not from the cold. *Hon*, the son of a bitch called her. Real cozy. And her with that lovey-dovey tone females use with a man who's poked them the way they like it.

His double-ten weighed damn near sixteen pounds loaded, and he hadn't lugged it along because Mattie was his target, not Fargo. Ace did have his short iron strapped on, but no gumption for shooting at a man like Fargo in the dark. That was an express ticket to hell.

Once again that lanky, woman-hogging bastard was *just* where Ace didn't want him to be. Another damn crusading do-gooder, only his reward wasn't bliss in heaven—it was pussy on earth. Ace's woman included.

Next time we meet, Fargo, Ace promised silently as Mattie joined her new stag, I'll have the field howitzer and you'll be rag tatters.

The freeze lifted early and fast, and by three hours after breakfast the sun began to feel pleasantly warm on Fargo's neck. He was still scouting, but in broken doses so he could return to the others often. And by noon he realized there was an ominous new source of trouble: a lone Nez Percé sentinel, riding well behind the celerity wagon.

"How long's he been riding drag?" Fargo asked Snowshoe.

"Chucky seed him first, 'bout a half hour ago. War watch, this child reckons."

Fargo nodded. When battle was imminent, tribes often assigned sentinels to watch any potential enemy in their home range. With mirror signals or smoke, sometimes using adolescent males as runners, they kept the main group informed on enemy locations and activities.

"This could get ugly," Fargo fretted. "Ain't been that long since I escaped a Sioux war party by the skin of my ass. How often can a man get lucky?"

"Hell, you seed them war boats on Lewis's River yestiddy," Snowshoe reminded him. "It's been a-comin' to a bile."

"Yeah. But I was hoping Ace and Duran would've made their next play by now, though, and we'd have them skinned and mounted on the wall. I expected a fandango at sunrise. I don't like dealing with both threats at once."

"Mayhap Ace and Duran are finally hanging up their hatchets," Snowshoe suggested. " 'Specially happens they got a good gander at their dead pard's blowed-off head."

"Possibility, I s'pose. But I won't bluff on it."

"Rather ride a mare," Snowshoe agreed. "Chucky's had more palaver with some Palouse pard o' his we met. Swift Canoe, he called him. They's Nez Percé runners all over the place, delivering knapped flints to the clan houses to make arrah points. Comin' down to the nut-cuttin', hoss."

Fargo nodded. "And the last thing we want to have hanging over us is wondering what Ace and Duran will pull next, and when. All along we've played this on our terms, and that's how we'll keep playing it. I've been studying on a little plan. Come sunrise, old son, what say we lance this boil?"

16

The sun broke over the jagged peaks of the distant Bitterroot Range, revealing an amazing sight to the gazes of Ace Ludlow and Jack Duran.

"Sweet mother of God," Ludlow said. "I *see* it, but I don't credit my own eyes."

He and Duran had tracked Fargo's party all day yesterday, after they left the thermal springs, to see where they'd camp next. The two had been awake since an hour before sunup, moving ever-so-cautiously into position behind a clutch of granite boulders. It wasn't too far from a circle of stones that marked the cooking fire.

The plan was to ambush Fargo and the old geezer while they were smack in the middle of breakfast, food in their hands. Ace's double-ten cut a wide swathe of destruction, and the loss of a couple of women was acceptable now. It wouldn't be impossible that one blast would take out half the bunch.

But during the night, others had beat them to it.

The celerity wagon lay tipped over on one side, partially burned. Female clothing and other possessions were scattered about everywhere as if a twister had gone through. But most stunning of all to behold: Fargo, the old coot, and the fat Indian all lay dead in the grass. Their bloody bodies bristled with arrows. There was no sign of the women themselves anywhere.

"Well, Jack," Ace finally said, "this explains all the shooting and whooping we heard last night. Looks like the Pierced Noses beat you to him."

"Took our damn women, too. Including your Mattie."

Ace grinned at that thought. "High-bred Matilda Everett

of Fairfax County, Virginia, being topped by flea-infested savages. Won't the newspapers and dime novelists eat *that* up when we sell it to 'em?''

The two men emerged into the camp clearing.

"The Injins beat us to him, all right," Duran said, sliding his razor from the sheath on his belt. "But can you imagine what the big, bad, legendary Trailsman's face and scalp will fetch, on display back in St. Louis, at ten cents a pop?''

Ace nodded. "*Hell*, yes. And one dollar gets you a tintype to show the grandkids.''

"I can cure and tan the skin before it shrinks too much. That bastard thought it was so damn funny when he ruined my ear. Now who's laughing, Fargo, you son of a bitch?''

Despite this tough talk, it was a mark of their respect for, and fear of, Fargo that both men moved in cautiously, even though their enemy was obviously long dead.

Ace clicked back the hammers of his double-ten. "Soon's you're done skinning him, Jack," he said, "I'm blowing the carcass into wolf bait. I swore he'd get a load, and by damn, he will.''

Jack knelt and reached forward to make the first cut. An eyeblink later, the "dead" Fargo rolled hard and fast to his left, jerking a length of twine that had been covered with dirt and tied to his wrist.

About twelve feet in front of Ace and Duran, catching them both flat-footed, the brush cover of a cleverly disguised blind was snatched back to one side by the twine.

And, all in a moment, Ace was staring directly into the muzzle of a one-pounder cannon. His own gun was useless because it lay in the crook of his arm, muzzle pointing off to one side.

"No!" he screamed. "Don't—''

Mattie, her pretty face determined, lowered a glowing rope to the cannon's touchhole. The powder charge ignited in a tremendous, belching roar, and sixteen one-ounce musket balls exploded in an incredibly destructive battering ram of lead.

Ace Ludlow caught the brunt of it. His face was instantly reduced to a red smear, his body torn to ugly gobbets of flesh unrecognizable as human. They lay scattered in the grass with the smoldering bits of wadding.

Jack Duran, however, had been kneeling and caught only one ball—which literally ripped the heart out of him. And ironically, Fargo realized when he sat up, shooter in his fist, Duran had died with his eyes wide open.

Snowshoe and Chucky leaped up, whooping in triumph, and thumped each other. The arrows sticking out of them were Ruck-a-Chucky's crooked "show arrows," cleverly rigged into their clothing. It was rabbit blood smeared all over them. And the racket Ace and Jack heard last night was just the three men busting caps and hollering war whoops to mimic the sounds of an all-out battle.

The well-heeled women had all been huddled in the overturned conveyance, which the men had already carefully tipped over before lowering them inside. Fargo had even scorched parts of it for authenticity and to cover the burning smell of Tammy's fuse rope. With the men's help, the gals climbed out now, Yvette flashing plenty of scarlet petticoat.

Ace's double-ten had been destroyed in the blast. Fargo had been fearing that "consequential" gun of his all along. So he had decided on a duel of formidable guns. And clearly, this time the biggest gun won.

He next looked at the wide-eyed Duran. Fargo reached down and tossed Duran's hat over his face.

" 'I will not abide a staring corpse,' " Fargo quoted, his face a deadpan. "Maybe he read his destiny in the tea leaves, huh?"

"Both them-'ere meat slabs," Snowshoe opined, "will end their days as vulture shit. Did their mamas proud."

"Let's stop reciting our coups," Fargo suggested, heading toward the overturned wagon, "and light a shuck outta here. 'Pears we've busted up the Ludlow gang, all right. But the Nez Percés are on the scrap now."

"A-huh. Sentinel's gone, though," Snowshoe said.

"That can mean anything. Quick, boys, put your shoulders into it."

They heaved the wagon upright, then retrieved the hidden horses from a nearby ravine. While the women gathered up their possessions, the men harnessed the team into the traces.

"Don't forget," Fargo cautioned the other men after the women were seated inside the celerity wagon. "I counted plenty of men in Ace's gang when they swarmed out to the river to squash that fire. I figure there's maybe four, five more prowling around. Maybe they lit out of this region, but we'll assume they didn't."

He sent a stern glance at both men. "I'm riding out to scout. You two jackasses gonna make them women save your bacon again?"

Snowshoe scowled; Ruck-a-Chucky giggled.

"Watch out for the rest of the gang," Fargo repeated.

However, just past noon, Fargo crested a long divide between two valleys and realized the rest of the Ludlow gang, too, were now kissing the devil's ass in hell.

Vigilantes had caught the four men, no doubt recognizing some of their plunder. Fargo could tell, at a glance, that the men had first been drag-hanged before being propped up on display, lashed to wooden slabs jammed vertically into the ground.

A sign, scrawled on a board with charcoal, hung around the neck of one man: FATE OF ALL BEDROLL KILLERS.

Couldn't have happened to a nobler bunch of knights, Fargo thought as he rode on. The dead were the dead, literally behind him now. But those Nez Percé smoke signs, rising from a bluff west of the Snake, suggested there was still hard slogging ahead.

For three days they tracked the Snake River north, drawing nearer to Lewiston—a place Fargo definitely intended to bypass, not only because of the threat from Nez Percé warriors, but because of the threat to five beautiful and lust-inspiring females. At Lewiston the Snake River jogged left, and it would be a much easier journey west to Fort Walla Walla if they followed the federal supply road.

But Fargo couldn't figure out the present situation with the Nez Percés. They had indeed begun raiding on the trespassers, raising one hell of a ruckus. But thankfully, so far the tribe had decided to simply harass them and run them off, not kill them.

Except, Fargo noticed in pure astonishment, they're completely ignoring us. In fact, a war party had just passed them and cheerfully waved!

"It's got this child some buffaloed, too," Snowshoe admitted when Fargo stared at him, astonished.

Both men were riding on the box for the moment, their mounts tied behind. Ruck-a-Chucky, riding flank, called over to them: "No trouble with Nez Percés. Chucky fix it good."

"How?" Fargo demanded.

Ruck-a-Chucky looked ashamed and glanced off toward the mountain peaks to the east. He was avoiding Fargo's probing, lake-blue stare.

"Chucky had plans to go back and steal the outlaws' gold later," he admitted. "But the war signs came. So then Chucky spoke with his Palouse friend Swift Canoe. He told Swift Canoe where to find the tunnel and cabin. Where to look for gold, too. White men always think the floor is safe. Swift Canoe is a good man. I saw his smoke signal for Chucky just now. All is good. He took the stolen gold and gave it to Chief Running Antelope. Our tribute payment. We will not be attacked."

"Cuss my coup!" Snowshoe swatted the big Indian affectionately, almost knocking him off the saddle. "You corrupted the big chief, you slyboots."

Fargo grinned. This was one time he would forgive Ruck-a-Chucky's scheming mind. In fact, the arrangement was only fair, Fargo figured. That gold was stolen from the tribe, and Running Antelope was a decent enough fellow. He'd maybe pinch off a little for himself, but he would also see that most of the money benefited the entire Nez Percé people.

"Chucky," he said, "you coulda left us at any time, took that gold, and hightailed it outta here. But you chose to stick, help your friends, even lose the gold. I'm glad I helped you beat the rope that time in the Sierras. You're a good man, underneath that scheming hide."

The Modoc's promise held true. Fargo's odd assemblage of travelers turned west, a few miles outside Lewiston, and found relatively good terrain through the Columbia Plateau, just now greening up.

"There it is, ladies," Fargo finally announced to their passengers as they reached the summit of a hill overlooking the log fort in the distance. "It's late enough we best camp here, ride in fresh tomorrow. With all those eligible bachelors that collect at a frontier fort, you'll want to look your best."

He sat his Ovaro beside the right-hand side windows of the conveyance. All five women had poked their heads out to gaze down at the fort. Now they stepped out, assisted one by one by Fargo.

"I'm always happy to turn a man's head, Skye," Mattie confessed with a smile. "But now that I'm free of my fear of Ace Ludlow, I'm going back East to attempt a reconciliation with my family."

"Ain't much to look at," Tammy said, meaning the fort. "But I hear tell there's rich men hang around them forts, lookin' for pretty gals to marry?"

"Pretty? Hell, gals with teeth will do," Snowshoe told her. "And lovely things like you? Out here, cupcake, it's just as easy to marry a rich man as it is a poor one. That way, fellows like me and my favorite turd here got us a steady supply o' willing wenches. We ain't sensitive like 'em-'ere rich toffs, our peeders is always ready—"

"Whack the cork, you old fool," Fargo snapped. "Launder your talk around folks who bathe."

" 'Scuse me, ladies, sorry I said *peeder* like that and shocked ya's."

"I just might look for one of those rich fellers," Tammy mused, sending Fargo a pouty little smile. "But I'm glad we'll be camping here tonight, Skye. That way there'll be time for . . . proper good-byes."

Fargo didn't miss Yvette's concurring nod. He had a feeling this was going to be a sleepless night; the good kind for a change.

Yvette, for whom imagination's loom was always weaving something melodramatic, now gazed into Fargo's eyes and cast an audible stage sigh.

"Skye Fargo," she pronounced grandly, "you are one of those rare men whom bees will not sting. *Never* shall I forget you!"

This was too rich for Snowshoe's belly. He guffawed as he climbed nimbly down from the box, favoring his hurt side a bit.

"Honey, no offense. That lad's been bee-stung, snake-bit, crapped on by birds, and treated for clap so offen they call him Mercury's Child. But he'll do for a 'hero' in these parts."

After supper, while Fargo was softening up the dirt with his Arkansas Toothpick before spreading his groundsheet, he saw the twins head toward a tree-sheltered creek. It emptied into the Columbia, and Fargo had picked this spot knowing the women would want to freshen up. Snowshoe and Ruck-a-Chucky had gone out to picket the animals, and Fargo hadn't seen them since.

Hell, those two girls *like* being ogled, he recalled. And after all, if he did get lucky, he'd have enjoyed the entire set of five gorgeous women. Besides—a man couldn't help pleasantly wondering about two beautiful girls who did *every*thing together. . . .

But the twins had bathed earlier. This time they hadn't gone to the creek, but to the private little shelter, formed by weeping willow limbs, where Snowshoe had spread his robes.

Fargo did a double take when he peeked through the curtain of willows and spotted both blondes, naked as newborns, forming a cozy little sandwich with Snowshoe—wearing only his new red long-handles—in the middle!

The girls blushed at spotting Fargo, but didn't trouble to cover up.

"You horny old goat," Fargo marveled. "They'll leave you dead, old man."

"Ah, they'll both be limping come morning, boy," Snowshoe boasted. "It's *all* good, hoss, 'long as your snake still bites."

Both girls giggled. Fargo sighed as he watched two pairs of loveliness jiggle.

"Kin you b'lieve," Snowshoe asked Skye, "these tasty li'l' tidbits ain't never had a man yodel in their canyons before?"

Snowshoe grinned and flicked one of his beard braids.

"Now hoof it on outta here, pup, or what you see next will shame you for life."

By late morning the next day, the five women had been safely delivered at Fort Walla Walla. Now Fargo and Snowshoe, both bleary-eyed, had reined in atop a long rise overlooking the fort behind them. Ruck-a-Chucky had already headed west toward the Pacific Coast and his home in the Klamath Mountains of Northern California.

"Lookit there, Skye," Snowshoe groused, pointing toward the fort as he spat amber.

Men and goods were streaming through the gates both ways, and the rudiments of a town were already going up around the fort.

"Buncha flies around a molasses barrel," Snowshoe carped. "Makes me ireful."

Fargo nodded, but he saw it differently than his bitter friend. Some of these fledgling Americans had got an idea fixed in their minds, an idea quickly becoming the national dream: Somewhere there was a piece of earth that meant personal fulfillment. Some would find that fulfillment, others would spend their lives taming one spot only to move on to another.

He begrudged no man his dream. For fiddle-footed Skye Fargo, however, there was no dream of empire or desire for dominion over land. By choice he was the Eternal Outsider, always yondering, always plagued by the "tormentin' itch" to see what lay over the next rise.

The two friends were parting here. They swung down and bear-hugged, thumping each other hard.

"This child ain't one to slop over, Skye," Snowshoe said, his voice gruff. "Happens this hoss ain't above the ground next time you yonder out this-a-way, don't fret none. You and me'll broach a keg in friendship at the Final Ronnyvoo, boy. Now gi' me a grip."

Snowshoe stuck out his callused paw and Fargo took it. The next second, he was sailing through the air. Fargo landed hard on his back, and the tough old mountain man held him there with a boot on his chest.

"Augh!" he roared out in a voice as strong and lusty as the very heart of his nation. "The name is Snowshoe Hendee! My goldang pecker is so damn big grizz bears use it for a scratch pole! I've kilt Innuns, buff, panthers, grizz, and Mex'can lancers! Heaven don't want me and hell's afraid I'll take over! And God strike me dead now if there's a better man breathing than Skye Fargo!"

For a long time, after Snowshoe rode off on his swayback mule, still making brags, Fargo stood there watching a unique figure in American history slowly fade into the same landscape that was still breeding legends.

"To the *old* ways, hoss," Fargo said, with true admiration in his voice.

Then the Trailsman swung up into leather and pointed his bridle east, toward the serrated peaks of the Rockies.

LOOKING FORWARD!
The following is the opening
section of the next novel in the exciting
Trailsman series from Signet:

THE TRAILSMAN #278
MOUNTAIN MANHUNT

*1861, the remote and rugged Gros Ventre Range—
where danger came in many forms, and death was only
a heartbeat away.*

The sharp crack of a rifle brought the buckskin-clad rider
to a stop. Out of habit he lowered his right hand to his
Colt. Eyes the color of a deep mountain lake narrowed as
he tilted his sun-bronzed face into the wind. Three more
shots sounded, evenly spaced, then all was quiet again save
for the rustling of the trees in the brisk breeze and the
squawk of an agitated jay.

Skye Fargo was deep in the rugged vastness of the Rocky
Mountains. Hunting and raiding parties from several tribes
frequently crisscrossed the region. The Shoshones were
friendly enough but the Blackfeet and their allies were not.
Since Fargo did not care to run into a hostile war party,
he was about to rein to the west to avoid whoever had

fired the shots when he spied smoke from a campfire off in the distance to the north.

Fargo knew that no self-respecting warrior would make a fire that big. Only a white man would be so foolish. Which might mean whoever fired the shots was white, and possibly in trouble.

"Damn," Fargo said aloud, and reined his Ovaro north. If he had any sense, he told himself, he would leave the whites to fend for themselves and go on about his own business. But he couldn't help being curious.

Before him unfolded a winding valley lush with thick timber broken by random clearings carpeted by high grass, a paradise untouched by plow or ax. For days Fargo had been amid virgin wilderness rife with wildlife and natural splendor, his natural element, as he liked to think of it, where he was as much at home as a city dweller would be on the streets of any given city.

Fargo had gone a quarter of a mile when he heard voices and gruff laughter. Common sense dictated he not let his presence be detected until he was sure it was safe, so when he spied those responsible, he drew rein.

In the center of a large clearing lay a buck in a spreading pool of scarlet. On their knees in the fresh blood, two grimy men in dirty homespun clothes had begun the butchering. One had a scraggly beard which he tugged with blood-streaked fingers and loudly declared, "It's a fine one, Mr. Whirtle, sir. There should be enough here to feed half the camp."

Four horses stood in the shade of a towering pine. Three were saddled, the last was a pack animal. Beside them stood a pencil-thin man dressed in a hunting outfit that cost more than most ordinary folks earned in a year. He wore a rakish brown cap and his boots were polished to a sheen. Of particular interest to Fargo was the expensive English-made rifle held in a crook of the man's elbow.

"How long will this take, Link?" the man asked, removing the cap to reveal neatly combed and oiled black hair. "I want to be the first one back."

"Oh, no more than half an hour, Mr. Whirtle," Link said.

"We have to peel the hide, quarter the meat, and tie it on the packhorse."

Whirtle scowled and said, "There's a twenty dollar gold piece for each of you if you are ready to head back in fifteen minutes."

Greed brought grins to Link and his companion. "For that much we'll be ready to go in ten."

"I thought you would see things my way," Whirtle said smugly, and fished a pipe from a pocket. "Today is the day I beat Teague. I can feel it in my bones."

Fargo kneed the Ovaro into the open. It amused him that they did not hear the dull thud of the Ovaro's hooves until he was almost on top of them. Link and the other skinner sprang erect while Whirtle nearly dropped his pipe as he brought his rifle to bear. "Relax," Fargo said. "I'm friendly."

"Why didn't you speak up sooner?" Whirtle testily demanded. "I might have shot you from your saddle."

"You would have tried," Fargo said.

"Who are you, mister?" Link asked. "What are you doin' in these parts?"

Ignoring him, Fargo studied Whirtle's thin, sallow features. "Those shots of yours could bring every hostile for miles around down on your head."

"I dare say we can handle them," Whirtle declared, patting his rifle.

"Just the three of you?"

Whirtle wedged the pipe stem into a corner of his mouth. "Our party numbers thirty-one, counting the cook and Teague's manservant. Thirty-five if you count the women." Whirtle advanced and offered a pale hand that had never seen a callus. "Garrick Whirtle, of the New York Whirtles. Perhaps you've heard of us? My family's business interests span the continent."

"Can't say as I have," Fargo admitted, wondering what so large a party was doing in the middle of nowhere. "This isn't New York. And it's no place for women."

"We have it on reliable authority that we are in no danger whatsoever from the savages who inhabit these wilds,"

Whirtle said stiffly. "Every member of our party has a rifle and a brace of pistols and we have enough ammunition to stand off an army of primitives."

Fargo said nothing. Arguing would be pointless. Many whites shared Whirtle's outlook, and only learned the truth at the point of an arrow or a lance.

Link came toward the stallion, his blood-drenched knife in hand. "You never answered my question, stranger. Who in hell are you and what are you doing in this neck of the woods?"

"I'm passing through," was all Fargo would say.

"That's not good enough," Link said. "It could be you're up to no good. Could be you're fixin' to rob Mr. Whirtle and his friends." He planted himself next to a stirrup and glared. "So you better start talkin' before I pull you off this critter and pound you into the ground."

Fargo kicked him. He moved his boot only a few inches but it was enough to knock the arrogant jackass back a few steps.

Shocked disbelief registered, and Link put a hand to his cheek. "Did you see that, Charley? This bastard up and used his boot on me!"

"I saw," said his friend, rising with his own knife low at his waist. "And if you want to haul him down and carve on him some, I'll back you."

The man called Whirtle, Fargo noticed, made no attempt to stop them, but stood watching with an amused smirk on his face. Link took a menacing stride, raising his knife to stab, and just-like-that Fargo had the Colt in his hand and thumbed back the hammer. "I'd think twice were I you."

The color drained from Link like water from a punctured bucket and he stood with his thick lips moving but no words coming out. Beads of sweat sprouted on his brow and he slowly lowered his arm.

Charley also froze but fingered the hilt of his knife as if he contemplated throwing it.

"Drop your blades," Fargo commanded, and when they obeyed, he lowered the Colt's hammer and twirled the revolver into his holster, then shifted toward Whirtle. "Nice of you to lend a hand."

Whirtle laughed and gestured. "Haven't you heard? This is a free country. Everyone has the right to be as stupid as they want to be."

Fargo wondered if that referred to Link or to him. "I'd like to know why you and all these others are here."

"Would you indeed?" Whirtle's smirk widened. "Why should I answer your question when you wouldn't answer Mr. Link's? He could be right. Perhaps you are a scoundrel up to no good."

"Suit yourself," Fargo said, lifting his reins. "But if your hair ends up hanging from a Blood or Piegan lance, don't say you weren't warned." He started to wheel the Ovaro but turned to stone when Whirtle suddenly trained the hunting rifle on him.

"Not so fast. I deem it best for our guide and Teague to have a talk with you. So I must insist you do us the courtesy of accompanying us to camp." Whirtle's finger was curled around the trigger, the hammer pulled back. All it would take was a twitch and the heavy-caliber rifle would blow a hole in Fargo the size of an apple. "That is, if you don't mind," Whirtle sarcastically added, and snickered at his joke.

Fargo was fit to slug him, but under the circumstances he smiled thinly and said, "I don't mind at all."

"Mr. Link," Whirtle said. "Relieve our visitor of his firearms."

Grinning eagerly, Link scooped up his knife and made to comply.

"No," Fargo said.

Link stopped and glanced at Whirtle, whose thin eyebrows arched in bemusement. "Oh really? And why should I let you keep them?"

"Because even if you put a slug in me, I guarantee I'll put one in you before I go down," Fargo vowed.

Wagging his knife, Link declared, "He's bluffin', Mr. Whirtle. No one is that fast. I say you should just blow the buzzard to kingdom come."

"East of the Mississippi River they call that murder," Whirtle said evenly, "and in case you haven't heard, it's against the law."

"But there are no laws here," Link said, bobbing his double chin at the surrounding forest. "Folks kill other folks all the time and get away with it." He winked and chuckled. "Who's to know, eh?"

"Am I to take it you have indulged on occasion?" Whirtle asked.

"How's that?" Link said, and blinked. "Oh. I get it. Well, let's just say that if you let me gut him for kickin' me, it wouldn't be the first time I've indulged, as you put it."

"Interesting," Whirtle said, more to himself than to them. "But I'm afraid Teague wouldn't approve, and the last thing I want is to make him mad. We'll keep this stranger alive for the time being."

"Whatever you want," Link said, unable to hide his disappointment. Muttering under his breath, he turned back to the buck.

Whirtle came closer to the pinto, the muzzle of his rifle trained on Fargo's chest. "You must forgive the simpletons," he said so only Fargo would hear. "Like most of our hired staff, they don't overflow with intellect. But someone has to perform the many menial chores required, and it certainly won't be me."

"You don't want to get your hands dirty, is that it?" Fargo asked, giving the man a taste of his own sarcasm.

"Why should I, when there are always lowly mules like Link to do the labor for me?" Whirtle let out a long sigh. "I hear comments like yours all the time. But I can't help it I was born into one of the wealthiest families in the state of New York."

"You're a long way from home."

"That I am," Whirtle said. "Teague is always taking us off on one grand adventure after another. Last year we spent a month in Africa. The year before that it was India. Next year, he's talking about South America."

The rifle barrel had dipped toward the ground as Whirtle talked. Fargo could easily kick free of the stirrups and tackle him, or draw the Colt and pistol-whip him across the head, but Fargo was content to lean on his saddle horn and say, "I take it you do whatever this Teague wants?"

Whirtle shrugged. "I suppose you could say that. We've

been best friends since we were old enough to walk. When we were little he always decided what we did, which games we played, that sort of thing. Nothing much has changed. You'll understand better when you meet him."

Link and Charley were carving on the buck with brutal zest. After peeling the hide, they cut the meat into sections but left much of it unclaimed, enough to feed Fargo for a month if the meat were smoked and salted. "You're wasting a lot of good venison," he commented.

"It's only a deer," Whirtle said. "I must shoot five or six a day."

"Your party eats that much?" To Fargo it seemed like an awful lot. But before the Easterner could answer, loud chattering arose from a tree at the clearing's edge. A gray squirrel had stumbled on them and was venting its irritation.

Whirtle glanced up, smiled, and snapped the rifle to his shoulder. He barely took aim. At the sharp *crack*, gun smoke spewed from the barrel and the squirrel tumbled head over tail from the limb to strike the hard earth with a flat thud. It twitched a few times, then was still.

"Did you see that?" Whirtle said. "Dead center in the head at forty feet. Not bad, if I say so myself."

Fargo had seen better. Most frontiersmen could do the same at a hundred yards and would not think it exceptional. "You shot that squirrel for no reason?"

"It annoyed me," Whirtle said. "Besides, what difference does it make? One less squirrel in the world is no great loss."

"It is to the squirrel." Fargo liked this man less by the minute. "Are you at least going to skin it and take the meat back?"

"What for?" was Whirtle's reply. "We have the venison, and all I'm after is my share."

"Your share?" Fargo said, but again they were interrupted, this time by loud crashing in the underbrush and the arrival of three more men on horseback. Two were stamped from the same coarse mold as Link and Charley, and one of them led a packhorse over which a dead doe had been tied. The third rider wore an expensive outfit similar to Whirtle's and had a large hunting rifle slung across his back. He was younger than Whirtle by a good ten years, his face as round and smooth as a baby's.

"Garrick! We were on our way back and heard your shot."

"You should keep on going, Jerrold," Whirtle said. "For once one of us can get the better of Teague. I haven't heard his gun go off yet."

Jerrold reined up and took an interest in Fargo. "Oh, I don't care who wins. For me the fun is in the hunt itself." He paused. "Who might your new acquaintance be?"

"He hasn't favored us with the information," Whirtle said. "I thought it best to take him to camp so Beckman and Teague can decide what to do with him."

Fargo straightened. "Beckman? Sam Beckman? Is he the guide you mentioned a while ago?"

"Yes. Do you know him?"

Quite well, Fargo thought to himself. Beckman was an old-timer who literally knew the Rockies like he did the back of his hand. A former trapper and mountain man who now made his living as a scout and guide, Beckman could still drink most anyone under the table and hold his own in wrestling matches with upstarts Jerrold's age. "We're old friends."

"Then he'll be pleased to see you, laid up as he is," Whirtle said.

"What happened to him?"

Whirtle opened his mouth to answer when suddenly more loud crashing erupted in the undergrowth, and the next moment into the clearing barreled the terror of the Rockies, a beast so formidable, a brute so savage, it was the one creature held in fear by all others: a grizzly.